I've Already Forgotten
Your Name, Philip Hall!

BETTE GREENE

I've Already Forgotten Your Name, Philip Hall!

PICTURES BY
LEONARD JENKINS

HARPERCOLLINS*PUBLISHERS*

Here's to my friends,
true, blue, and funny too,
Pierrette Francis and Marian Hershenson
— B.G.

Library of Congress Cataloging-in-Publication Data
Greene, Bette, 1934-
I've already forgotten your name, Philip Hall! / by Bette Greene ;
pictures by Leonard Jenkins.—1st ed.
p. cm.
Sequel to: Get on out of here, Philip Hall.
Summary: Beth Lambert, a teenaged girl who lives in the small town of
Pocahantas, Arkansas, experiences the ups and downs of friendship with
members of the Pretty Penny Club and best friend Philip Hall.
ISBN 0-06-051835-9 — ISBN 0-06-051836-7 (lib. bdg.)
[1. Best friends—Fiction. 2. Friendship—Fiction. 3. African Americans—
Fiction. 4. Arkansas—Fiction.] I. Title: I have already forgotten your
name, Philip Hall!. II. Jenkins, Leonard, ill. III. Title.
PZ7.G8283Iv 2004
[Fic]—dc22   2003013830
Typography by Amy Ryan
1 2 3 4 5 6 7 8 9 10
❖
First Edition

1 'Bye, 'Bye, Walnut Ridge   1

2 Howdy Do, Pocahontas   12

3 Please Don't Go Away Mad   19

4 I've Already Forgotten
   Your Name, Philip Hall!   33

5 The Case of the Missing Piglet   46

6 The Elizabeth Lorraine Lambert
   & Friend Detective Agency   60

7 The Pocahontas Patriot   78

8 Beth's Bad Luck, Terrible Day   88

9 The Great Arm-Wrestling Contest   99

10 The Piglet-sized Lie that Grew
   and Grew and G·R·E·W!!!   110

11 And the Winner Is . . .   125

12 The Patriot and the Pirate   142

13 The Fun Maker   153

1

'Bye, 'Bye, Walnut Ridge

Not until she swung the last of those brimming-over-with-apples wooden crates onto the truck's rear platform did my grandmother stop to wipe a bit of sweat from her forehead. "Used to be I'd load my truck front to back without so much as sweating up a drop," she said, while giving her forehead a quick swipe with the sleeve of her flowery dress. "Must sure be getting old."

What a strange thought! At the same time that I knew all grandmothers are old, I somehow still couldn't believe it. I mean *really* believe that my very own Mama Regina was getting old. "You getting old? Why, everybody says you're Walnut Ridge's best volunteer firefighter! And not even your hired man can lift a single one of those crates onto this truck without struggling, straining, and sweating, and remember Sidney Earl ain't even seen the last of

1

his teens. Now, ain't that the truth?"

I watched as her gray head bobbed ever so slowly, first up and then down, and I could just tell that she was thinking. I could tell that she was thinking of something that happened so very long ago. And as we walked back into the house, she began her out-loud remembering. "Reckon I wasn't even as old or as strong as Sidney Earl is now when your granddaddy up and died. Lordy, I felt so bad, missing him like I did. Oh, it was sad, what with your own mama just a sweet little baby, crying in her crib.

"That's when I figured that I didn't have no choice in this world, but to get strong or to get poor. Somebody had to pick the apples, put them into crates, load them onto the truck, and drive them to market. Somebody had to make us some money. Yes siree, and that somebody wasn't nobody but me. Nobody but skinny little me to take care of my farm and my pretty, little baby girl—your mother!"

Although I had never seen her eat or drink anything any more magical than Dr. Booden's ugly tasting cough medicine, still and all I thought I'd tell her what folks hereabouts are all-the-time saying. "Some folks in Walnut Ridge say you've got yourself some very secret SECRET that you keep all to yourself. Some secret that you've never told, 'cause only somebody with either a magic medicine or maybe some magic words could be as strong as you are."

"Ha!" she answered, as she served me up a thick slab of honey-baked ham and half a platter of her really crispy-crackly okra. It wasn't until she set herself down in front of her own plate of ham and okra that she said "Ha!" once more. While she reached for a square of cornbread, I waited patiently. At least patiently for me, which probably ain't very patient at all, but even so, she still didn't say another word. Well, maybe that was only 'cause she was drinking buttermilk. A person probably needs food in her belly before she goes telling secrets, especially very important, magical secrets.

After what seemed like a very long while, but was probably only a very short while, I figured that she wasn't going to say anything more than "Ha!" So, I had to come right out and ask her what I've been wanting to know for all these weeks I've been living here with her in Walnut Ridge. Why, any minute now Ma and Pa will be driving up that dusty road to bring me back home to Pocahontas, and I might never get a better chance to ask than now.

I listened while the okra made loud, crunching sounds in my mouth. "Well, how do you reckon you did it, Grandma? If it's not magic, then how come you don't just up and tell folks how you did it? Just got so strong?"

Suddenly the wrinkles across her forehead wrinkled more deeply. "What you talking about, girl? Is you saying that I'm keeping secrets?"

"Well, the truth is, folks are say—"

"And I've told you more than once not to go listening to what folks in Walnut Ridge, Arkansas, be saying, 'cause if they said only what they know to be true, then most folks wouldn't hardly be doing a speck of talking!"

"But if they don't know," I protested, "then that sure don't keep them from suspecting this or suspecting that. Folks say that all the time Grandpa lived, they never saw tiny, little you lifting anything heavier than your seven-pound baby. But folks sure sat up and took notice after Grandpa died. Why, both the Mulhern brothers tell how they looked out their window one morning and saw you pushing your loaded-with-apples truck five miles into town after the motor broke down."

The old lady shook her head so hard that her dangle earrings struck back and forth against the side of her face. "I don't care what them Mulherns go around saying! The motor didn't fall out till I reached the highway, so I didn't have to push that truck no five miles! Four miles maybe, but five miles never!"

"Well, maybe," I said, hoping not to get her all excited again. "If you could just tell everybody how you got strong enough to push a loaded truck four miles, then folks would stop asking, stop pestering, and finally stop wondering."

Mama Regina sighed just as though this explaining was going to be real hard work, a heap harder work than lifting up apple crates or even pushing her broken down truck. "If I've told one person, I've told a dozen people, and some of them I've told more than once. Fact is, most folks don't much like the truth 'cause the truth is hard, but magic—well, magic is easy. With magic everybody can get everything they want anytime they want it by sprinkling a little stardust, making a wish, or saying silly stuff like *Abracadabra*.

"Well, I don't believe in none of that stuff. No siree bob. I believe in the truth, and so that's the only thing I'm going to tell you. Only thing, I is only going to tell you once, sweet Bethy. Only one time and never, ever again."

I nodded okay, while all the time feeling honored beyond belief that I was at last going to learn the secret of my little grandmother's extra-big strength.

"The secret of my strength," she said, looking at me with the kindest eyes of chocolate brown that I've ever seen, "is that it ain't a secret."

"You mean it ain't?"

"No."

"Well, nobody knows. Nobody understands how you do what you do."

"Well, just the same, it ain't no secret and it ain't no magic."

"Then what? What is it?"

My grandmother laughed just as though the joke was on me. "Oh, Bethy, sweet Bethy, you is sure enough filled with confetti. Why, the answer is plain, as plain as that there crumb of cornbread hanging onto your lower lip."

I swiped at the crumb with a paper napkin. "If it's so plain then how come I don't know? How come nobody in all of Walnut Ridge knows?"

"Same reason that you weren't really listening to me, girl, when I already done told you that it ain't stacks of stardust or even something out of a magician's mysterious sleeves that gives me my strength. No, Beth, what I did didn't take a smidgen of magic, it only took a plan and work. Working long and hard to build up strength, little by little and day by day!"

I shook my head at the wonder of it all. "Imagine that," I said at last. "The secret that all of Walnut Ridge was looking for and wondering about was all the time right there in front of their noses. Every bit as plain as all those little red apples just a-hanging from your trees."

Then, from outside the house, I heard the gravel on the driveway crunch under the moving weight of a vehicle. "Ma and Pa! They're here! Finally, finally, I'm going home again!" But only one glance at my grandmother's face and I knew that my too-enthusiastic words about leaving her had soured her spirits. "I'm sorry! I didn't mean that I don't love you, and didn't love being here with you, 'cause I do; I only meant that I've been missing my home, missing it badly. That's all I meant."

Her expression changed from sour to sweet, and I could tell that all was forgiven. And that's when I thought, hoped, wished that the Pretty Pennies, the best girls' club in all the world, would also be forgiving. Forgiving enough to forget what I did wrong. Forgiving enough to welcome me back home!

When I heard gravel crunching on the driveway, I jumped up and looked out the window, expecting to see the dusty, old Lambert truck. Only it wasn't a truck at all, but the big, black, shiny car belonging to my friend B. J. Faulk—or, at least, to the father and mother of my friend B. J. Faulk.

"Look, Mama Regina, look! It's B. J., Millie Mae, and Specs, all the girls of the Irritated Oysters Club," I said, as the car with Mrs. Faulk at the wheel backed up and sped away.

My grandmother's head bounced up and down just as though their surprise visit didn't surprise her a bit. "Betcha they're coming to say good-bye and to thank you for showing them how to start that girls' club, the Invited Oysters, that makes fun for the whole town. Betcha they're all coming to thank you, 'cause thanking a person is the right thing to do."

"Uhh . . . only we're not the Invited Oysters, Mama Regina, we're the *Irritated* Oysters. 'Cause if you irritate and annoy an oyster they'll make a pearl."

"Reckon that's exactly what I said," replied a really irritated Mama Regina. "The Irritated Oysters!"

Even before the girls had a chance to step upon the

porch, I had swung wide open our front door. "Sure am happy you all dropped by, 'cause I sure didn't want to leave Walnut Ridge without saying good-bye to the three best friends that I made in this town."

But one glance, that's all it took, just one glance to see that something that should have been there (like a smile) was nowhere to be seen. No, not even the born-smiling Millie was wearing a good-bye smile for me. Even so, I called out, "Howdy," but those three Irritated Oysters looked as though they were way too irritated to howdy me back.

My grandmother waved them in. "Go sit yourselves down at the kitchen table, girls, so I can serve you all up pieces of my world-famous razzle-dazzle pie." They did what they were told, and after awhile they actually broke into big, broad smiles, but I think it had more to do with Mama Regina's pie than it had to do with me.

For more minutes than a few, the Irritated Oysters ate pie and brought cups of chocolate to their lips that was too hot to drink, but not too hot to sip. And although they talked, they only talked among themselves. Why, I just might as well have been the doorknob, for that is how much (or actually, that was how little) they talked to me.

I was feeling miserable. Unwanted, unneeded, and yes, unloved. How come they're now treating me the very opposite of the way they use to treat me? How come on my last day in Walnut Ridge they're suddenly treating me so bad? Not like all those other days, when they were all the time asking, "What do you think of this, Beth?" and "What do you think of that, Beth?"

I looked first at B. J. then Millie Mae and finally at Specs before asking, "If there *is* something wrong—I mean if you all are mad at me, then why don't you come right out and tell me why?"

B. J. stared at me through eyeglasses as thick as her thumb before answering, "Well, as if you don't know!"

"Well, I don't know."

"Yes, you do know."

"I guess I oughta know what it is that I do know and what it is that I don't know. And what I don't know is why you all are mad at me."

Mille Mae asked, "You mean you really don't know?"

I nodded. "I really don't know."

"Then I'll tell you," agreed Specs. "You're leaving us. You're going back to Pocahontas and taking all the good times with you!"

B. J. added, "Yeah, you're going back to that terrible town where they had a secret nighttime meeting and stole the presidency of the Pretty Pennies away from you. Right when you weren't looking and didn't expect it."

"Well, you're right about that," I admitted. "I sure didn't expect it, but maybe I should have, seeing as how I got to be too bossy, too big for my britches, and so I reckon I don't blame them for what they did. Not a bit!"

Then all three girls were talking at the same time, all telling me that I've a "sworn and sacred duty" to finish up all the fun I started. "Don't you have any loyalty? Aren't we friends, Irritated Oyster friends? And besides, how can you go back to *that* place that didn't treat you right? How can you leave this good place for that bad place?"

Although I waved my hand for quiet, I didn't know what I was going to say, at least not exactly. So I started, "Well . . . you are all my friends, my very good friends." I told them, "Without you all, I would have been alone and friendless in a strange new place.

"But please don't say bad things about the Pretty Pennies, 'cause what they did—what happened—wasn't their fault. It was mine. Back then I figured that because I was the best at making good times happen, then, then I was like some kind of princess that everybody had to obey.

"Well, maybe that's what I thought back then, but it sure ain't what I think now. Reckon that right here in Walnut Ridge I learned that I ain't nobody's boss. So now it's time to go back to a place where I ain't never gonna be no visitor. I'm going home to the big P—back to my home in good ole Pocahontas, Arkansas, U.S.A.!"

2

Howdy Do, Pocahontas

The evening stars glittered and twittered in a cloudless sky as our pickup truck, with me squished and squashed between my mama and poppa, sped past the familiar black-and-white road sign: WELCOME TO POCAHONTAS, ARKANSAS. *A historic river port town overlooking the Black River.*

With Pa's right arm dropped around one shoulder and Ma's left hand dropped around my other shoulder, I could tell that I was going to be hugged all the way home. But because I didn't want my folks to think that all I've been worried about was Philip Hall and the Pretty Pennies, I didn't ask a single one of the questions that I longed to know, like, Has Philip Hall asked about me? and, Are the Pretty Pennies having the time of their sweet lives now that Bonnie Blake is their new president?

But almost from the beginning of the ride, Ma began warning me of danger. "You stay away, far, far away from them now out-of-jail butchers, 'cause both Calvin Cook Senior and Calvin Cook Junior ain't stopped complaining that they never would have gone to jail in the first place if it weren't for you. You and Phil Hall sticking your noses where they didn't belong, in other folks' business!"

"Don't worry, Ma."

"You just remember that them evil butchers don't think you're a hero. No siree, 'cause they is still mad, madder than a queen bee robbed of her honey. And the good Lord knows that there just ain't never no telling what evil folks as evil as them might do. So no more investigating mysteries. Keep on remembering that detective work was never meant for girls. You hear me a-talking to you, Beth?"

"Oh, don't you go worry none, Ma."

"*Oh, don't you go worry none, Ma,*" she mimicked. "Well, that's just fine and dandy for you to say. You go seven miles up the road to your grandmother's, and everything is different. Feels like something that should be a part of me has been ripped away, and suddenly what should be a part of me ain't a part of me no more. Never in all my born days was I sadder to see someone go," she said, giving me a hug with a strength that I never knew she had. "And never in all my born days was I happier to see someone come back home again."

Just at the spot on the highway where Pa turns off onto the narrow dirt road leading to the Lambert Farm, I smiled the moment I saw our familiar, but faded sign:

1 mile

↑

Lambert Farm
good turkeys
good pigs

But the very next thing I spied was something I had never seen before. Pointing, I said, "Hey, would you looky there at that big, new building! What is it? A store? A bus station?"

Pa's laugh came from deep within his belly. "OOOeeee-Weee! A whole army of workers been working on that for weeks now. All the time that you've been away."

"But what is it? And how come you can't keep from chuckling, huh, Pa? 'Cause whatever that huge thing is, it sure looks nice."

Since Pa couldn't quit his snickering, it was Ma who came up with the answer. "That's the new home of Mr. Putterham."

"You don't mean *our* Mr. Putterham? That miserable and miserly merchant of the Busy Bee Bargain Store?"

"Same one. Same old tightwad who's so stingy he rubs the picture off a nickel," answered Pa, who now seemed to be aiming for every rut in our old, rutty road. "The storekeeper comes along and builds his palace next to our pig and turkey farm, and now what do you think he's doing? Complaining (folks say he's even crying *real* tears) 'cause he says our pig farm smells like a pig farm. Well, how in heaven do you reckon pigs oughta smell excepting the way that pigs *do* smell?"

In the next minute we reached the spot where the road rises, and that's when I can see, at the far end of our headlights, our home, our wonderful home, painted a nice pale green.

"Your sisters and brothers don't want to wait one second longer than they have to. And since you've been away, we've been mighty worried about our baby. Problem is, Baby Benjamin has stopped trying to say real words, no, not even *Mama* or *Poppa*," said Pa, as the truck began wildly circling around and around our house, while he rhythmically struck the truck's horn with his fist. *Toot-te-TOOTTOOT . . . Toot-te-TOOTTOOT!*

"Want to know something, Mr. Eugene Lambert?" asked Mama, as the circling truck leaned us first this a-way and then that a-way. "Sometimes I knows that I've got four children, but when you act like this, I'd swear to goodness if I ain't got five!"

As soon as Pa cut the motor, I raced toward our house

until I reached the front steps, and then with a flying leap, landed at the front door just at the moment that it swung open. And then it was arms . . . arms, all those loving Lambert arms pulling me inside.

Annie, my fancy Annie of a big sister, wrapped her arms around me, and then bouncing straight up in the air like a ball, she jumped back down to wrap her arms around me once more. But the really surprising surprise was my big brother, Luther, who had never been seen actually hugging another living creature (except maybe his prizewinning pig, Miss Beth, and her baby, Baby Beth, the world's only singing piglet). All the same, Luther did something really peculiar. He hugged me. ME!

And all the time he's hugging, he's explaining, "And as soon as Baby Beth is ready to sing before an audience, you're gonna be the first to hear her."

I asked my brother, "How is she coming along with her singing lessons?"

A worried look went rolling across his forehead. "Oh, her singing is in tune alright, but the problem is the words. Sometimes Baby Beth just up and forgets the words."

I glanced down to see what was tugging on my jacket, and that's when I saw those pudgy little arms stretching up toward me. I scooped him up, twirled him around and around while he squealed with delicious delight. And my baby brother didn't even wait until we quit our whirling and twirling before slobbering a very wet and runny howdy-do kiss on my cheek.

"Baby Benjamin, how come you won't say *Mama* or *Poppa*?" I asked. "How come you won't even do that?"

But he only smiled wide enough to show off his teeth—actually, tooth. He only had one.

"Oh, come on now and be a good boy and say *Ma-ma* . . . *Ma-ma*."

His eyes brightened as his lips formed a perfect O, and I could tell that this time he was really going to say it, finally say his very first word. "Come on, little man, I know you can do it. Just say *Ma-ma* . . . *Ma-ma* . . . say *MA-ma!*"

Our family circled around the littlest Lambert, 'cause nobody wanted to miss seeing and hearing an event that can come only once in a person's lifetime. A person's very first word! When our baby noticed how very interested everyone was in his performance, he let his O-shaped lips thin out into one single smiley line. And then, without saying anything, he just giggled. Giggled and gurgled just as though the joke were on us.

"Okay, Baby Benjamin," I said, while trying hard to keep in mind that folks always have to be very, very patient with babies. "If you're not ready to say *Mama*, then would you please, oh please, pretty please say . . . *Pop-pa*. Come on now and say after me, say *Pop-pa* . . . *Pop-pa* . . . *Pop-pa*."

For one shorter than short moment a smile danced across his sweet lips before he went ahead and did it. He said his very first word so loud and so plain that even a deaf person couldn't help but hear it. 'Cause he didn't say it just once or even twice, but three times, he said, "Beth . . . Beth . . . Beth!"

3

Please Don't Go Away Mad

When I heard that noise coming from our kitchen, I looked around to see which one of us Lamberts was making all that racket. But no, everybody is right here with me, right here in the living room. And it wasn't just noise that I heard either, it was voices. Real people's voices! But whose?

"Well, what's—who's that?" I asked, just as the kitchen door swung wide open and all them pretty-as-a-picture Pretty Pennies came parading in. Was it them, really, really them, or was I only dreaming just another one of my happy-ending dreams? I willed myself to wake up, but when that didn't help, I pinched one finger and then another. But that didn't work either because, miracle of miracles, I already was wide, WIDE awake!

Reckon all my fears about my Pretty Penny friends

being mad and staying mad were just that, nothing but my foolish fears. So it was really real, just like I always dreamed and schemed it would be. My friends, all my very pretty Pretty Penny friends, are right here, welcoming me home. I guess what Mama Regina once told me is true: getting mad at friends don't mean that you've stopped loving them. Guess I'll never stop loving the Pretty Pennies, and now I know—know for the first time in a very long time—that they've never stopped loving me, either.

Leading them high-stepping marchers into our living room was none other than our new Pretty Penny President, Bonnie Blake, with one of them little red hum-a-zoos stuck firmly between her teeth. Closely following was the silent Esther, the gorgeous Ginny, and beating out time on a rusting Maxwell House coffee can was Susan the sweet.

As they circled me and my family, they were clapping and chanting in perfect rhythm. "Go, Pret-ty Pen-ny . . . Go, Pret-ty Pen-ny . . . Go, PRET-ty PEN-ny! GO! GO! GO!!!"

Then, at that same exact moment, all the Pennies came to a sudden foot-stomping stop before bending low and throwing themselves high into the air while shouting, "HOO-ray Beth!" Followed by a second jump while even more loudly shouting, "HOO-ray Beth!" Then the four girls did it a third time, only this time they leaped still higher in the air while booming out, "HOO-ray BETH LAMBERT! Hoo-RAY! HooooOOOOOOOO-ray!!!"

For a moment or more everything was quiet, and that's when Esther nodded toward me. "Well, don't just stand there, Beth Lambert, with your mouth flung open like some old mangy cat done stole away your tongue," demanded the one Pretty Penny who mostly acts as though some cat had permanently taken off with her tongue. "Well, for goodness sakes, Beth, go ahead and say something."

My first thought was to grab them all, hug them all, and thank them all for being my friends, because in spite of everything I did (or didn't do), they (believe it or not!) love me still. And because my second thought was just like my first thought, that's exactly what I did. I hugged them all so hard that for a moment I was afraid that I might squeeze the very life out of them!

But then, suddenly, Bonnie blew into the kazoo, and everybody kind of straightened up and shut up just as though kazoo blowing was pretty serious stuff. Since I didn't exactly know what it meant or what I was supposed to do, Bonnie was nice enough to explain. "As your new Pretty Penny President, I've been very busy, working very hard on our club rules."

"We've got . . . *rules*?"

Bonnie threw me a look that nobody could ever mistake for friendly. "I *heard* you say that!" she boomed.

21

"What?" I asked. "Said what?"

"You went right ahead and spoke while I, the president of the Pretty Pennies, was speaking."

"But . . . but, no, I only spoke," I tried to explain. "In that little piece of space when you weren't doing even a speck of talking."

"Under this *new* president," Bonnie shouted, while poking her finger hard against her own chest, so that nobody would ever have to guess which "new president" she was referring to, "we finally got ourselves rules. While you were over there in Walnut Ridge having yourself a good ole time on your grandmother's apple farm, I was busy working just as hard as I could work, making up rules. Do you have any idea how difficult it is to make up whole barrels full of rules, regulations, and laws?"

Ginny groaned, "Ain't nobody got more rules than us Pennies. We ain't got no freedom, but we sure do got rules, more rules than a ruler."

"We got us rules for standing," said Susan.

"We got us more rules for sitting," added Esther. "And we even have rules about when we can go to the bathroom . . . and when we can't."

Bonnie's eyes narrowed as though she was ready and willing to take aim at us all. "Don't for a minute go thinking that I don't work hard on my rules, 'cause I sure enough do. Ask anybody! Why, I make up lots and lots of rules every morning on the school bus on my way to school, and I make up even more rules on the school bus that takes me home!"

"We know," answered all the Pennies in weary unison. "Reckon we sure enough know!"

A now-annoyed Bonnie challenged, "Is there anybody who'd ever want to go back to those days when Beth was president? With everybody always a-joking and a-joshing and a-jollying around? And noise? Enough noise to scare away a whole mountain full of Gorilla Men! So who, in their right mind, would ever want to leave the quiet of our peaceful meetings to go back to all that, all that noisy confusion?"

Suddenly all hands (except Bonnie's and mine) went stretching high up in agreement. "Well, I would!" squealed Esther. "That's when things were always a-popping."

"I would too!" Susan quickly agreed. "'Cause the only reason boring Bonnie's meetings are quiet is 'cause we don't hardly make no noise sleeping!"

Bonnie threw her hands against her hips. "Oh, you is gonna burn in hell for your lies, Susan, truly you will!"

Ginny must not have been particularly worried about the burning-in-hell threat as she bounced her gorgeous head up and down, while all the time calling out, "Me too! Me too! Reckon we all want to go back to those noisy and exciting times when Beth was our president!"

"But . . . but I can't be your president, 'cause you've already got one," I told them. Actually, I kept telling

23

them that, but nobody paid me even the slightest bit of attention.

Mostly they were busy arguing with Bonnie as she went on explaining what a wonderful president she was. "You all better think hard before you try to get rid of me, 'cause unlike when you had your old president, since I've been your president, we Pennies ain't lost a single relay race against them Tiger Hunters. Why, we Pennies ain't even lost a single argument against Phil Hall and his sometimes nice and sometimes not Tiger Hunters. Now have we? Tell the truth!"

Sweet Susan didn't look one bit sweet as she snapped back, "Reason we ain't losing relay races is 'cause we ain't been relaying no races. What I learned after Beth went away is that there's something a whole lot worse than *losing* a relay race, and that is *not having* a relay race. And why we ain't, in fact, losing arguments with them Tiger Hunters is easy enough to explain. We ain't been talking to them, and they ain't been talking to us. So worse than losing arguments with Tiger Hunters is not having any words at all with Tiger Hunters."

Esther raised her hand for permission to speak at the same exact moment that she began speaking. "Do you think not talking to Tiger Hunters is fun? No, everybody knows that's no fun. Truth is, there ain't been no fun hereabouts, no, not a drip or drop of fun, not since Beth went away!"

All the while, poor Bonnie was looking more and more helpless. Made me want to help. "Well, peace and quiet can be right nice," I reminded the Pennies. "I mean, it's all so . . . so quiet and peaceful."

But even as I came to her defense, I saw that Bonnie was pointing a furious finger at me. She said, "Well, I guess that's the thanks I get for doing all the good things for you Pretty Pennies that I did do. And you—you, Beth Lambert, come strolling back here and you don't even say howdy good before you try stealing my presidency from me. Well, stealing is wrong and stealing is hurtful, and it's too bad that you don't know that!"

As I slowly and thoughtfully nodded my head, I felt the pain of remembering. "Reckon nobody has to tell me, Bonnie Blake, how hurtful it is to have your presidency stolen away 'cause it happened to me, and it happened to me first. Mine was snatched away from me at a meeting at your house. A meeting so secret that it was kept secret even from me!"

"But . . . but," Bonnie sputtered. "I wanted you to come to our secret meeting, honest I did. Only if you'd have come to that meeting then it wouldn't have been no secret anymore. Now ain't that so?"

As soon as she said that, all the other Pennies began arguing loudly with Bonnie. "No, it ain't so! You're the one, the only one of us, who wanted it secret, 'cause you're the only one who wanted to take Beth's job. You promised us that you were going to be a better-than-Beth president. But you weren't!"

Bonnie wiped at her eyes. "Well, if you all are too ignorant and too unappreciative to appreciate all the good things I've done for you, then you can let Beth be your president. See if I care! Only remember that things weren't always so peachy when she was our leader. So don't go thinking that all of Beth's ideas were good ideas, 'cause they weren't!"

"Bonnie, you sure are right about that," I told her.

Tearfully Bonnie went right on with her explaining. "Don't you all go forgetting about the time Beth had us working days and nights making all those fancy little paper boats. Remember how we put those secret messages hidden inside? And remember how she told us all we had to do was to set our boats down on the Black River, and sooner or later those boats would sail down our river before crossing an ocean, and finally landing on faraway distant shores? And then after a while (but not too long a while) people with brown skin and white skin and yellow skin would get our friendly messages and send us friendly messages right back. Remember Beth promising us that?"

On Esther's face, there was a faint smile and a dreamy look just as though she was remembering something good from long ago. "Yeah . . . those little paper boats," she said, "were sure nice."

The bossy one argued back, "Only they didn't cross no ocean, 'cause as soon as those paper boats got wet, they sunk straight down, down to the bottom of the Black River. And now, ain't that the truth?"

I answered, "Oh, Bonnie, you're sure enough right about that, too. How could any Pretty Penny president not know enough to know that paper can't keep water out?" And now, thanks to Bonnie, I remember still one more dumb-fool thing that I had forgotten all about. Probably never would have remembered about our decorated paper boats either if Bonnie hadn't been good enough to remind me. Reckon it just proves that I've made too many mistakes to remember them all. And what better proof do I need to know that I've made way too many mistakes to ever again be president?

Bonnie threw both arms into the air. "The paper boats were another one of Beth's bad mistakes, so I vote for me, Me, ME. The no-mistake, calm, and peaceful president. The one who made the rules when there were no rules and made regulations when there weren't no regulations! And laws? Why, I could talk on and on about all the laws I've made."

I raised my own hand. "I vote for Bonnie."

Even so, I was outvoted, 'cause it was Bonnie and me voting for her while the three of them voted for me. Next thing I knew, Susan, Ginny and Esther were talking about how very soon now we're all going to be happy 'cause "we're gonna be getting our fun back."

"I thank you all for wanting me, sure do," I said, while all the time shaking my head no. "But the truth is, I can't be your president."

The wails seemed to come from everyone, but it was Susan who spoke. "Well, how come, Beth? You still mad at us for our secret meeting? We told you we were sorry. Didn't you hear us say we were sorry? Didn't you hear us say that?"

I shook my head. "Nah, I ain't one bit mad at you Pennies. Fact is, ain't nobody more to blame for that than me. Always thinking I was right, always thinking I was too smart to be making mistakes, and then I started making them. One mistake, two mistakes, three mistakes, and MORE!"

The silent Esther's nose wrinkled up the way it always does when she's trying her hardest to understand what she can't exactly understand. "Well, if we're not mad at you, and you're not mad at us, then how come you won't be our president?"

"'Cause it's just not my time to be president, it's Bonnie's time, and taking her presidency away before her time is up is wrong. And anyway, maybe Bonnie will learn about being a leader from her mistakes . . . 'cause I know I sure learned a lot from mine."

Then it was Bonnie shaking an angry finger, first at the Pennies and then at me. "Guess you all heard it with your own ears. Beth coming right out and admitting she made mistakes, big, gigantic, humongous mistakes. And while I'm not one bit looking down on Beth, 'cause I may have even made a mistake, too, while I was president, but . . . but, well, the truth is, I don't really think so."

As soon as Bonnie said those words, all the Pennies began helping her out by remembering, and even numbering, each and every one of her presidential mistakes. And with each and every failure that the girls called out, Bonnie seemed to grow smaller and smaller, sadder and sadder.

And it wasn't just Bonnie that changed before my eyes, all the other Pennies did too. The sweet one, for example, wasn't looking all that sweet anymore. Fact is, she was looking like she had been raised on a diet of sour pickles. The gorgeous one was anything but pretty now that her mouth had curled down into a sneer. And the silent one was anything but silent as she shrilly accused Bonnie of being "not just the most boring, do-nothing leader in Arkansas but in the whole world."

Didn't they know? Couldn't the Pennies tell that they were making our friend, Bonnie, feel so bad? Somebody—anybody has got to lead the Pennies out of all their ugly faultfinding. But nobody said a thing except to go on remembering still more of good ole Bonnie's goof-ups, foul-ups, and screwups!

Then, at last, I heard it. A voice, a single voice, strong

and sure, calling out, "Leave her be! Please just leave Bonnie be!" I looked at first one Penny and then another to see just who it was that had enough leadership and courage to end Bonnie's pain. But what I saw was that all the girls were now focusing on me. Could it be? Well . . . yes, I reckon it must have been me!

Maybe I did okay with leading this time, but I can't hardly do it again, 'cause getting Pennies to shut up and behave themselves is the job of the president, and that's the one thing I'm not. And I'm way too scared about making mistakes to ever be president again.

Reckon that the Pennies, though, must have forgotten that I wasn't still their president, 'cause they all did exactly what I told them to do and left poor Bonnie alone. And they went on looking at me just as though I and I alone could tell them what to do next. And so that's what I did do. "Don't none of you ever forget that at that secret meeting, you all voted fair and square to make Bonnie Blake your president . . . so I think it's only fair and square that we Pennies just keep the president that we've got.

"But that don't mean that we can't help our president become a better president," I explained. "Help her stop pestering everybody about her rules, regulations, and laws so that together we can all do other things, more fun things!"

Bonnie bounced to her feet and began talking so loud

and furiously that her flying spittle sprayed like April showers across my cheeks. "So if you're going to go insulting my rules, Beth Lambert, then I'm out of here. So good-bye, traitor, good-bye!"

"But I didn't mean—," I said, but I didn't get to say another word 'cause Bonnie was already out the door. As it slammed behind her, I turned to the other Pennies, whose expressions already told me that they had all turned away from me. First Ginny, then Esther, and finally Susan spoke, but they all spoke about the very same thing. About giving me one more, my very last, chance to be president.

What could I tell them that I hadn't told them before? We can't go back to those sometimes-terrible times when I was doing so many things that always made somebody mad at me about one thing and somebody else mad at me about another thing. No, I didn't want to do that anymore, 'cause I wanted to keep my friends, *all* of my friends. And to do that I wouldn't do much of nothing, not one way or another way, then I'll keep my friends. 'Cause you can't hardly hate something that's nothing. Now ain't that right? Ain't that really, really right?

Esther had begun shaking her head so hard that at first I thought it might have been mounted on springs. "We, Pennies, come to you in our time of need, needing your leadership help, and you say no. What kind of friend would do that? No kind of friend all!"

All at once, the gorgeous one took Esther and Susan by the arms. "Let's go home. I don't want to stay here a minute more than I have to!"

"But wait! Please!" I called after them. "Can't you see—don't you understand that I'm doing nothing so that I can't make any more mistakes? And all this doing nothing means I'm doing nothing bad to you. So how can anybody in their right mind ever be mad about *nothing?*"

The only answer that they gave me was the thud of their footsteps out of our living room, onto our front porch, and into the distance. I watched the Pretty Pennies until they became hidden by the night. So I told myself once and then I told myself once more that Pretty Pennies never stay mad at each other, leastways not for long.

And that's when I told myself that I was absolutely, positively not going to cry . . . even as I did.

4

I've Already Forgotten
Your Name, Philip Hall!

The next morning we Lamberts did what we always do come Sunday morning. All shined up and spiffed out in our very best Sunday go-to-church clothes, we walked through those old wooden doors of the Old Rugged Cross Church. But this time something was different. Yeah, something was very different.

Seemed as though there wasn't a single head that wasn't twisting itself either this a-way or that a-way, trying to catch a better look at me. Mama bent her head low to whisper, "Now don't you go getting upset even more than you already are. It's only that folks have already heard that you came home from Walnut Ridge last night, and they've got themselves a little friendly curiosity that needs satisfying, and so that's all there is to that."

"Maybe, but still in all, it makes me feel like one of

them circus sideshow freaks."

"Why, you of all people ought to understand curiosity, Beth Lambert, 'cause the good Lord knows you were born with enough of it to kill ninety-nine cats."

As our family went sidestepping along the pew until we reached our very own seats, I whispered back, "Well, just the same, I sure wish they'd stop it. What do they expect to see that they haven't seen before? That I went and grew myself another head?"

Just two pews ahead of us were four Pretty Pennies sitting so close you'd think they were sewed together head to hip. It was easy enough to spot them, 'cause those four heads were the only heads that didn't bother to turn back to stare at me. Reckon they saw all they ever wanted to see of me last night. That's okay, let them be mad, if they want to be. If they think it bothers me, then they're wrong, 'cause it doesn't bother me at all! Reckon I'll get by, leastways as long as I can keep *him*, as long as I can keep my very best, best friend.

I oh-so-carefully sneaked a glance at the seat where I knew he'd be sitting, and there he was, just a-sneaking his own oh-so-careful glance at me. Then as quickly as the snapping of rubber bands, our eyes sprang back to where they belonged, looking down at our prayer books.

He saw me, actually saw me looking at him! I felt hot waves of embarrassment rushing over me. Well, anyway, what am I getting all upset about? Just because a girl is caught looking at one boy doesn't mean that she likes him, 'cause it doesn't mean much of nothing. Reckon everybody knows that. Or at least they should.

Sometimes I listened as Reverend Ross went on and on, sermonizing about the fires of hell and that glorious life without end inside those pretty pearly gates of heaven. Now, I'm not one to name names, but there are four girls that I know (and know quite well) who wouldn't know what do on a rainy Pocahontas afternoon without me. Leastways they wouldn't know what to do without me stirring up, mixing up, and cooking up some delicious little bits and bites of excitement. So if they should someday make it up to heaven, and I don't, I think they're going to have a terrible time finding something—anything—to do. Maybe those four now mad-at-me Pennies sure better hope (and a little praying wouldn't hurt either) that I make it up there to heaven too.

After church services, I said howdy to the Pennies, and, although they were all within reaching out and touching distance, they didn't see or hear me. Or at least they pretended they didn't. Maybe I couldn't ever make them like me again, but, at the very least, I could keep them from finding out how very sad it made me.

Well, I still had Philip Hall for a friend, and once he's your friend, you're never gonna be friendless. As he made his way toward the church door, I watched the sunlight touch his face. And I wondered if anywhere on earth there was a prettier face than his. But now that I see him, what in the world should I do? Should I go rushing up to him the very moment that he steps outside? Or (and this is important!) would it be better to wait until, kinda natural like, he drifts on over to me? And I know for an absolute, positive fact that he *will* wander on over—or, at least, I . . . I reckon maybe.

As my family made their way toward our parked truck, my pa waved me on. "Come on, girl, get the lead out of your pants! 'Cause in honor of your homecoming, your ma is gonna serve up all your favorite eats: tamale pie, fried turkey, floradora potatoes, and heavenly hash. I can hardly wait!"

"You all go on ahead, Pa. My feet—well, for some reason, my feet just feel like walking."

He smiled a knowing smile before hopping behind the wheel and driving off toward home in a storm of dust. I followed the dust bowl that Pa's fast-moving truck kicked up until the vehicle was out of sight, and then, after a while, even all that stirred-up dust slowly settled back down to earth.

I've been walking for a while now. Shouldn't that boy have caught up with me? Could I be walking too fast? Now, that's really dumb! Only thing faster than Philip Hall's feet is Sheriff Nathan Miller's siren-squawking squad car. Nope, ain't nobody can walk faster than the long-legged president of the Tiger Hunters' Boys' Club of

Pocahontas, Arkansas. And that's a fact! Then, if that's a fact, and it sure *is* a fact, where-oh-where could that boy be? I thought of one reason why he wasn't with me, but that was too hurtful a reason to even think about, so I didn't think about it!

But . . . but could he be with her? No, he could not be with her! He wouldn't, not in a zillion and one years, be walking with a certain gorgeous Pretty Penny (whose name I will forever keep secret). No, no, a thousand times NO! And that's just way too-too ridiculous to think about!

To prove to myself just how happy I was, I laughed out loud, but it wasn't what anybody would mistake for a *real* laugh. My laugh reminded me of the laugh that people hereabouts laugh whenever they try to pretend that they're not afraid of Gorilla Man, who some folks swear is still living up there inside one of those caves on Pinto Mountain.

Then I thought I heard something from behind—something like the thud of a footstep on the hard, dirt road. This time I felt myself smile an honest-to-goodness *real* smile. Ohhhh, so that's it. That boy is trying to fool me by sneaking up from behind.

Well, just watch while I fool him before he fools me. I made my face and hands as scary as a werewolf's before suddenly twirling around on my heels while screaming, "GOTCHA!" But to my big surprise (and even bigger disappointment) Philip Hall was nowhere to be seen, 'cause there wasn't nothing or nobody there.

Those hurtful thoughts that I had only a moment before pushed away were now pushing back, and pushing back hard. Now I was talking to myself, talking real loud and real mean. "Well, let him walk Ginny home! Do you think I care if he walks the gorgeous one home? No! No! No!!! Let them walk till their foolish feet fall off, and you think I'd care?"

I wasn't so much walking home now as I was *storming* home, kicking gravel here, throwing stones there. And all the while yelling loud enough to carry all the way up to the top of Pinto Mountain. "Why, I wouldn't care if I never again heard the name Philip Hall! Not ever! Why, he's nothing but a low-down, no-good polecat with a low-down, dumb name!"

"Well . . . hel-lo, Beth Lambert."

I twirled to my right, but nobody was there, so I twirled to my left, but nobody was there, either. Then a familiar voice called from overhead. "Most of the time you'll find us no-good, low-down polecats up here in trees, Beth!"

And when I looked up, I saw him—Mr. Philip Marvin Hall in person—hanging from the thick bough of an old pecan tree. I didn't know which would be better, dying from the pure pleasure of seeing him again, or dying from the pure embarrassment at being overheard acting exactly like I felt. Jealous and mean and mean and jealous!

"... Uh, well, I reckon I didn't know you were here—I mean there," I said, while wondering if I had ever before in all my life said something so plain that it didn't need saying at all. 'Cause who in their right mind would ever say what I said if I had known that he was there? All my jealous rantings and ragings!

I looked around for some bottomless pit (a really deep well would do) for me to fall into, but I didn't see one. I started remembering something that folks say when they get embarrassed. They say they could have died from embarrassment. I wondered if it was true. Then I thought how lucky I'd be if only that would happen to me.

He swung down to ground level. "So I reckon you is back." And then, like it was the most natural thing in the world, he fell into step with me.

"Reckon I is." And although I could tell by the look on his sweet face that he had things to tell me, and I surely had things to tell him, we both just went on walking without talking. After a while, I heard myself speaking up, "All that spouting off, I did . . . guess I was a little upset, thinking that you weren't my friend no more."

Philip smiled his most adorable smile, and that's when I remembered why he'd always be the cutest boy in the J. T. Williams School and the bravest Tiger Hunter of them all. "Ohh, I'm your friend alright," he told me. "I'm your *best* friend. Sure am." And he said that as though it was the most natural thing in the world to say. "Only I didn't know—not till I heard you being jealous over Ginny—that I was your best friend, too."

I answered in a voice that wasn't much more than a whisper. "I reckon . . . I reckon you are, Philip Hall."

Way too soon to suit me, we had walked to the spot where the old rutty road forks. Follow one branch to the Lambert Turkey and Pig Farm or follow the other branch to the Hall Dairy Farm.

"Well, I reckon I'll be leaving you here," he announced, just as though it were big news to me.

"Reckon you will," I answered, sounding a whole lot sadder than I meant to sound.

Suddenly he flashed his winningest smile. "Hey, Beth, have I been interrupting you?"

"Interrupting me?" How come he didn't know that for some minutes now we've both been doing a tub full of thinking, but neither one of us has done more than a thimble full of talking? "Interrupt me from . . . from what?"

He gave a running kick at a clump of earth, "Oh, I was just thinking. . . ."

"Thinking about what, Philip?" I asked, as my eyes took in that sweet, sweet face. To say that it is a handsome face would sure enough be saying the truth, but still it wouldn't be saying nearly enough. Skin the way God intended skin to be, the color of milk chocolate with

40

maybe a tad of yellow sunshine mixed in. And a smile that told everybody who saw him that here was one fellow who was just happy to be alive and well and Philip Hall.

". . . it's nothing, nothing important," he mumbled while staring straight down at his still shiny church-going shoes.

"Then tell me anyway what's not important!" I said, while all the time knowing that it had to be something mighty important.

"Nothing is important. Not important, nothing is. . . ." Then slowly his face lit up like Christmas tree lights. "Only I was thinking that if you wanted to ask me something then there sure ain't no need to be shy so . . . so go ahead and ask away."

If Philip Hall wanted to confuse me, he was sure enough doing a good job of it. "Well, sure I will," I told him. "I'll go ahead and ask away . . . only I don't know what it is that you want me to go asking away about."

Then, as unexpected as a bolt of summer lightning, he grabbed me around the waist, and we suddenly went do-si-do-ing around and around the alfalfa field. Around and around we danced with nothing for music except our laughter and the squawking of the crows. "That's to remind you," he said when we finally slowed to a stop, "that I come from a long line of dancing fools."

"Ohh, so that's it? You want me to invite you to the

Pretty Pennies' once-a-year, every-year, Swing-Your-Partner Barn Dance?"

"Now you is talking sweet music, Beth."

"But, well, the thing is that Bonnie is the new leader of the Pretty Pennies, and she didn't say a word, nary a word, at our meeting last night about this year's Swing-Your-Partner Dance."

"Bonnie Blake? Are you going to stand there with your mouth open telling me she's the Pretty Penny president? Don't you think I know better than that? Everybody knows better than that, 'cause that girl ain't got enough leadership ability to lead ants to cookie crumbs."

"Hey, don't go talking bad about a Pretty Penny president. You don't hear me talking bad about the Tiger Hunters' president, now do you?"

"Ain't nothing bad you could say about the Tiger Hunters' president," he said, poking hard at his own chest and looking at me as though I was trying to fool him. "'Cause everyone already knows that I'm the president, and the bravest Tiger Hunter of them all. Are you saying that you're not going to invite me to be your partner? But who? Who else is there to invite?"

All the while I was shaking my head, trying to explain that I don't know nothing about no Swing-Your-Partner Dance, he was looking at me. Actually staring at me as though every moment that passed, his suspicions were growing more and more suspicious. Then, all at once, and with squinting eyes, he asked, "What'll you think I am, some dumb dummy?"

"Some what? Why, no. . . . I never—"

"You just a-keeping me a-flipping and a-flapping in the wind like a flag on a flagpole, waiting for an invite to the dance while you all the time got yourself a new Walnut Ridge fellow!"

"What *are* you talking about, Philip?"

"OHHhhh-HO! Think you can fool me? You can't fool me, Beth Lambert, 'cause I'm on to your tricks!"

I shook my head. "Maybe you know what you're talking about, Philip, but I *honest-to-goodness* don't know what you're talking about!"

"What I'm talking about is you going and inviting some dumb and nutty Walnutter instead of me!" For the first time ever, I noticed that as he spoke, the vein on the side of his neck was pulsing on and off, like the flashing neon sign over the Busy Bee Bargain Store. "Ask anybody and they'll tell you that Walnut Ridge folks are so dumb that they think watermelons grow on apple trees, and so weak that they can't tie their own shoelaces! Nothing but a whole town full of weakies and wobblies! Reckon everybody knows that."

"I *don't* know that!" I shouted back, thinking of all the good people of Walnut Ridge. Who was he to lie about people I loved. People like Mama Regina and my friends, all the girls of the Irritated Oysters.

"Yeah, well, I betcha the nutty Walnutter you invited is so weak that you'll have to sit him down and rest him between dances."

"He will not!"

"He will so!"

"Will not!"

"Will SO!!!"

"Will NOT! NOT! NOT!!!"

Philip's neck vein was really popping. "Will SO!!! Will SO!!! WILL SO!!!"

"You are really wrong, Philip Hall, and now I just might tell you why you've got everybody saying you're the bravest Tiger Hunter of them all."

"I say it 'cause I *am*. I am the bravest Tiger Hunter of them all!"

"Nah, around these parts we've got us deer, bear, razorbacks, and wild turkeys aplenty, but the one thing that nobody has ever seen around here is . . . tigers! And want to know what I think? I think it's as easy as pie to be brave about something we ain't got!"

"Well . . . well, if I met up with a tiger, I wouldn't be afraid, not a bit! If I'm brave enough to be the best arm wrestler at the J. T. Williams School, then I'm sure brave enough to be the bravest tiger hunter of them all. It's almost the same thing!"

I corrected him. "Is not. It's very different, and besides, that boy that I'm thinking about inviting is such a great arm wrestler that everybody calls him 'Cyclone.' Although Cyclone ain't his real name, only that's what they call him: Tyrone the Cyclone."

Suddenly Philip looked so sad, and what he said next made me feel sadder still. "Boy, I bet you weren't over there in that town more than a week before you had already up and forgotten my name."

But just as I was opening my mouth, ready to tell him the truth, that I could never live long enough to forget his name, he said something that made my sadness go away and made my madness come roaring back. "Yeah, well, you go tell that nutty Walnutter that I hereby challenge him to an arm-wrestling match! For the sacred honor of the Tiger Hunters and our town, I will wrestle him down. You go tell that to poor ole weakly and wobbly Cyclone Tyrone."

"You're sure right about one thing, Philip Hall, and sure wrong about another thing."

"What am I wrong about?"

"You're wrong about the Cyclone being weak and wobbly."

"Well, what am I right about?" asked Philip, beginning to look a little hopeful.

"You were right when you guessed that not even a week had gone by before I had already up and forgotten your name, Philip Hall."

5

The Case of the Missing Piglet

Poor Baby Beth! Poor little Baby Beth!" The voices were yelling and screaming, but the more I listened the more I could tell that it wasn't only God's voice. It was the angels, too. And over and over, the voices kept asking me the one question I couldn't answer. How come, they wanted to know, I went through a whole lifetime without having a single friend to call my own? No, not one Pretty Penny, and not even one especially special Tiger Hunter, either.

If I looked to my right, I could see the sweet, soft glow of those pretty pearly gates, but if I looked to the left, there were those fiery flames. Flames hot enough to roast a jillion marshmallows. OHHhh, NO! Hell was so close that I was now feeling the heat.

"Oh, poor, poor little Beth!!!" Suddenly my eyes

popped open, and the bad dream was only that, a bad dream. "Poor, poor Beth, little Baby Beth!" Only my name really was being called out, though not at all by heavenly folks, but by my all-too-earthly big brother.

Rolling out of bed, I followed the angry cries of Luther into the kitchen, where Pa was trying his best to calm him down. "Rushing up on Pinto Mountain with your shotgun ain't no way to get your singing pig back, Luther. Now, it just ain't."

"But, Pa, don't you see?" he pleaded. "I've got to do something right away before . . . before the Monster of the Mountain gobbles up Baby Beth for his midday snack."

Pa shook his head wearily before pointing to the rack of keys that hung on the kitchen wall. "Hand me them truck keys, Luther. This is something that's too big for you and me to do alone. Let's drive into town and talk it over with Sheriff Miller."

They started out the door when my pa suddenly stopped short as though he had just thought of something he had almost forgotten to tell us. "Muddy footprints we found outside the pigsty are way bigger than this," he said, spreading his hands as wide as the kitchen door. "So you all stay in the house, no matter what! 'Cause if Gorilla Man has got it into his head to eat our piglet for a snack, then there just ain't no telling what else (or who else!) he might get it into his head to eat for dinner."

After Pa and Luther left, we were all a little nervous and a lot scared, so I came up with a plan. Annie kept lookout toward the front of the house. I kept lookout toward the back of the house, while I told Ma that she had to cook up everything in the house that was cookable. Because at first sight of the Monster of the Mountain, we were gonna leave all her good cooking for him to eat and run. We were gonna run for our lives!

After we were at our lookout posts for a while, my fancy Annie of a sister rushed back to my kitchen-window lookout. With hands shaking and tongue stuttering, she said, "I th-think I see-e something mm-moving behind the t-trees."

Holding my hand so tight that the blood stopped flowing, she pulled me to the living room window and pointed a trembling finger toward that big, old oak tree. "Look!" Annie exclaimed. "There, right there below our tree house—something is moving! Ain't something mm-moving?"

"Yep," I answered, while giving calming little pitty pats to her shoulder. "Something sure enough is."

"Gor-Gor-Gorilla Man?"

"No, not Gorilla Man. Only a deer and her little doe."

I went back to my lookout at the kitchen window in time to see Pa's truck hightailing it back home. In the next minute, Pa and Luther, wearing their very bravest looks, strode into the house. Pa looked at Ma and told her that she shouldn't worry none, "'Cause, I'm not worried."

Ma brushed her flour-coated hands against her flowery apron before answering, "Don't go telling me not to worry, Mr. Eugene Lambert! Just tell me what dangerous dang-fool thing you is fixing to do. Least that a way, I'll know what I'm not supposed to be worried about."

"Go on, Pa, tell her!" encouraged Luther.

"Yeah, Pa, tell us all," I said.

He cleared his throat and looked over at Ma, as though begging her to understand what he already knew she wasn't going to understand. "Well . . . the sheriff is asking every able-bodied man in Pocahontas to get his gun and join him in the search for the Monster of the Mountain. So, since Luther and I are about as able-bodied as you can get, we're joining the sheriff and his posse up on Pinto Mountain."

"Luther?" Ma repeated, as though she was hearing her own son's name for the very first time. Suddenly, she shook an angry finger at Pa. "You is a grown man, Eugene Lambert, and I ain't your mama, so I can't stop you from risking your own sweet life against that evil giant. But, I *am* that boy's mama," she said, while pointing to Luther, "and he's got to mind me when I tell him that he's way too young to go searching for Gorilla Man."

"I *ain't* too young!" my older brother squawked. "You tell her, Pa. Tell her that I ain't one bit too young!"

Slowly, Pa shook his head no. "This time, Luther, I reckon your mama is right. Fact is, you *is* too young.

Better stay home with Baby Benjamin and the women folk, and I'll do what I can—anything I can do to save your precious piglet."

Now it was Luther who was shaking his head no, only he was shaking it fast and furiously. "Pa, I have to go, 'cause *not* going goes against everything that you've ever taught me."

Pa blinked. "It does?"

"Oh, yes sir, it sure enough does! Wasn't it you who taught me that a man takes care of what belongs to him? How a *real* man gotta be responsible for his family, his home, his animals?"

"Well, yes, son, but—"

"Then I reckon you can understand how it makes me feel," Luther interrupted, "to stay safe at home knowing that all the men folk from all around are risking their lives on that mountain to save my piglet. My own, sweet Baby Beth! So don't you see? Can't you understand? I've got to do my part, honest I do!"

After Luther and Pa (carrying their shotguns over their shoulders) left the house, Ma told Annie and me to get dressed up like it was Sunday, 'cause where we were going was praying. By the time we walked through the familiar doors of the Old Rugged Cross Church, the place was getting pretty well filled up, mostly with women folk who had come to pray for the safe return of their men from Pinto Mountain.

Then, suddenly, the quiet became still quieter as Reverend Ross, wearing black robes and a deep and troubling frown, strode to the pulpit. For longer than a moment, he just stood there glaring at us without speaking. Nothing, not a single word! All of us worshipers were silent, almost too nervous to even breathe, 'cause we all knew that something was coming. Only nobody knew exactly what or when.

Then, without even a wink of a warning, our preacher threw his arms heavenward as he cried out, "I am mad! Oh, am I mad!"

From the back of the church, a woman's voice rang out, "Well, whatcha mad about today, Reverend?"

That's when he began explaining about being in town today when the sheriff was calling for all the brave and strong men of Pocahontas to, once and for all, join in the search to hunt down the Monster of the Mountain. Our preacher told us how he interrupted the sheriff, telling the men that, no, they didn't need to go searching, 'cause what they needed to do—all they needed to do—was pray.

Amid shouts of "Amen . . . A-Amen," Reverend Ross went on to explain. "Our God is a big God. Big enough to take care of this Gorilla Man and all the Gorilla Men that was and all the Gorilla Men that ever will be."

Before very long, though, I had stopped listening to our preacher and began silently listening to all the thoughts that went tumbling around and bumping about my brain. Something was not right! But what? What wasn't right? Then it struck me. I mean, if all the men were busy searching Pinto Mountain and all the women were busy praying, then who was busy investigating the crime of the missing piglet? I asked my question and then, in the very next moment, I answered my very own question. Nobody!

It's been a while since Philip and I have been detectives, but, hey, it wasn't that long ago. And the sign that I once painted to advertise our business is still leaning up against the side of our barn. That's the sign that reads: THE ELIZABETH LORRAINE LAMBERT & FRIEND DETECTIVE AGENCY. WE SOLVE CRIMES. LITTLE CRIMES IN A LITTLE BIT OF TIME. BIG CRIMES TAKE A LITTLE BIT LONGER!

With all our good detective work, it didn't take Philip Hall and me very long to solve one of Pocahontas's most mysterious mysteries. The case of the missing turkeys—that was our most famous case. But that was back then Philip was my friend, but he sure ain't my friend now, and just maybe he'd never be my friend again. And when I thought about that, my tears came so quickly and unexpectedly that they went flooding all the way down my cheeks.

By the time we returned from church, I had figured out what I needed to do and the one person that I had to do it with. I didn't even know if he would, I only knew that I had to try. So I sneaked out of the kitchen door and began running. I raced down our farm road, crossed the fork in the road, and followed the sign's arrow:

But it wasn't until I peeked inside the open barn door that I saw Philip lifting a heavy set of dumbbells. Again and again, lifting it up and putting it down. For awhile I stood there and watched, 'cause I hadn't untangled my thoughts well enough for talking.

At least not yet, 'cause I needed to first come up with just the right "eraser" words. Reckon my mama taught me about some of those wonderful words that can rub out all the hurt feelings between friends. She taught me that when I wasn't much more than five or six. Oh, maybe seven or eight.

Boy, wouldn't just the right eraser words come in handy now to erase that patch of bad-mad feelings that have grown like a forest of stinkweeds between us. Only problem is that the eraser words I'm now remembering, like "Please" and "Thank you kindly," don't seem like exactly the *right* eraser words for this oh-so-sad situation.

Then it happened that Philip Hall looked up from his barbells and was now looking straight at me. But he couldn't be looking! Not yet. Why, I wasn't ready, 'cause I hadn't yet decided what to say . . . or do.

His face, his sweet face, was not showing that he was my true and sworn enemy, but then again, it wasn't exactly showing that he was my true and sworn friend, either. I took a few nervous steps forward. "Howdy, Philip."

"Howdy, Beth."

So we were *still* speaking! Me to him and him to me. That was good. One step and then another, I was walking toward him. "Whatcha doing, Philip?"

For a long moment, he looked at me right funny. Just as though I was asking a question that didn't hardly need no asking, but even so, he went ahead and answered it anyway. "Girl, how come you don't know curling—arm-wrestling training—when you see it?"

"Arm-wrestling . . . training? Well, why? I mean, well, what for?"

"What FOR? You standing there with your tongue wagging in the wind asking me the dumbest question I ever have heard."

But being the sweet boy that he sometimes is, he went ahead and answered it. Sort of. "Where you been resting your mind? Otherwise you would have already known what everybody in this here town already knows;

Pocahontas ain't won a single baseball, basketball, or football game against those low-down, good-for-nothing Walnut Ridge teams in nine years. *Nine* long years!"

"But, Philip, that's easy enough to explain. Their teams are better than ours, and that's all there is to that!"

In all the years that I've known him, I've never before feared that the top of his head might go blowing off, but I was wondering if maybe that might happen now. Sometimes, I know for a true and honest fact, I say things that are wrong, but there was no doubt right now that what I just said might not be wrong, but it sure was upsetting.

He was shouting at me something about the honor of the people of Pocahontas, and most important of all, he said, was the honor and good name of the Tiger Hunters. "I and I alone must avenge the honor of the Tiger Hunters! That's why our Mayor Potter has written a letter to that mayor over in Walnut Ridge challenging Mr. Fancy Pants, Tyrone the Cyclone, to an arm-wrestling, do-or-die, Saturday duel with me."

This time I thought it was *my* head that might go blowing off. "Ohhh, no, Philip! NO!"

"Well, what's wrong with that?"

"Everything," I told him. "Just everything."

"Well what? What?"

I closed my eyes, hoping to find a believable excuse that I couldn't find with my eyes wide open. And finally

I did. "What's wrong is Saturday. Saturday, that's what's wrong."

"Saturday is too a fine day," Philip protested. "That's the day when the farmers come into town for the gossip and the news."

"Well. . . ." I answered, making that a very long word. "I happen to know that it's not a good day for the Cyclone."

"How come?"

"It just ain't."

"How come it ain't?"

"Well . . . 'cause . . . 'cause that's the day that the Cyclone polishes his shoes. Got to look his sunshiniest best, you know, for the next day. For Sunday, when he goes to church."

"Oh, Beth, you got a basketball-size hole in your head."

"Make fun of me if you want to, Philip, but the problem is that nobody in our town will be dumb enough to watch a boring old arm-wrestling contest when there are lots more interesting things in Pocahontas worth watching."

He fastened his arms to his hips. "Yeah? Name something more interesting than arm wrestling for the championship."

"Lots!"

"Name them!"

"Ohh, well . . . there's checking out the windows of the Busy Bee Bargain Store for pretty things . . . there's looking at the pictures of movie stars behind the glass cases at the Pocahontas Picture Show, and there's also . . . there's. . . ."

"Told you so! Told you so!"

In my most disgusted voice, I told him, "It's really hard to think when somebody keeps interrupting your thoughts!"

Philip threw his head up. "Ain't nothing going to be more exciting for the Pocahontas folks than to see me bring back all the honor and glory to our town, and that's a fact!"

"But I didn't come here to talk about arm wrestling, 'cause I came here to talk about something important."

"Arm wrestling *is* important."

"What I mean," I explained, "is that I came here to talk about something . . . something else that's also important. Philip, do you know where all the men folk are? Do you know where they are right here at this minute?"

"Why, sure I do. They is all up there on Pinto Mountain fixing to gun down the Monster of the Mountain."

"That's right, but that ain't right, 'cause . . . 'cause it ain't right to shoot an *innocent* monster."

Philip went back to lifting up his dumbbells. "You can't prove he's innocent."

"You can't prove he ain't."

"But . . . but," he sputtered, "the piglet *is* gone!"

"That don't prove the Gorilla Man stole it."

Philip Hall shook his head no. "That don't mean he didn't."

"Well, if Gorilla Man steals, then how come he's never stolen anything else? Not in all these years that he's been hiding up there from the circus folks? So, now I guess you understand what we gotta do. Right, Philip?"

With firecracker energy, he shook his head yes. "Right. Right!" But in the very next moment, it looked as though his brains were getting all clouded over with confusion, before asking, "What? What is it we is fixing to do, huh Beth?"

"Why, naturally enough, we is fixing to investigate," I told him. "Together we detectives of the Elizabeth Lorraine Lambert & Friend Detective Agency are going to solve the mystery of the missing Baby Beth!"

6

The Elizabeth Lorraine Lambert & Friend Detective Agency

As Philip and I trudged around and about the muddy pigsty, searching for the evidence that would show us who dunit, he suddenly stopped short. "How come we is sloshing around hunting for clues when everybody and his brother already knows for sure and for certain who done stole the piglet?"

"Maybe they know," I answered, while bending over to pick up a bubble-gum wrapper. "But then again, maybe they don't."

"Know what I think?" he asked, but without giving me time to respond, he went ahead and answered his own question. "I think for sure it was that monster up on Pinto Mountain, but if it wasn't him, then I know for sure what happened."

"You do?"

"Why sure."

"What you aiming to do, boy, tease me or tell me?"

"I'm aiming to help you out here. All you gotta do is think. Think, Beth Lambert, think about that poor little piglet with all them boring singing lessons. Morning and night, singing lessons, while all those other piglets all the time be teasing Baby Beth because she's different. And Baby Beth, what does she want? Does she want to be a singing star? Nahh, all she wants is to be normal like everybody else. Left alone to be a nice, normal piglet that's happy oinking and oozing around in the mud all day."

"Philip, you have to be kidding. Tell me, *are* you kidding?"

He made a face as he examined the squishy mud that rimmed his shoes. "I ain't kidding. I think Baby Beth was so unhappy that she ran away from her home—I mean away from her pigsty. All those lessons, and all that teasing from the other piglets got her so upset that she just up and ran away from home. You want to know what I think? Well, that's what I think!"

In spite of myself, I heard what Philip Hall must have surely heard: my low groan of disbelief. And I could tell that hearing that made him good and mad. "Are you going to go around with your nose scraping mud, Beth, and tell me that I'm wrong?"

I came up to my full height. "No, Philip, I'm going to

look you full-square in the eye and tell you that you is wrong. Really, really wrong!"

"Well, if it wasn't Baby Beth running away from the pigsty, then it was probably something else," Philip answered with real conviction, as he leaned up against the fence post and fell into what looked like deep thoughtfulness. For a while all was quiet, as Philip leaned and I searched, until, suddenly, he had a bright, new thought. "Ohhh, *now* I know who stole Baby Beth!"

And because he sounded so certain, I couldn't wait to hear. "What—who? Who stole the piglet?"

"Betcha you're glad you got me here to figure things out for you, eh, Beth?"

"Reckon you know I am, Philip," I said, 'cause it was sure fine having Philip Hall as my friend, whether he figured things out for me or not.

He shook his head, disgusted like, as though he didn't understand how a person could be as dumb as me and still make it through a day. "How come you didn't catch on, 'cause it was as plain as the mud on your nose!" He laughed and slapped his thigh at his joke, all the while I rubbed pigsty mud from the tip of my nose.

"Why don't you just tell me?" I asked, showing my annoyance at being the butt of his not-all-that-funny joke.

Philip explained, "What people do once, they'll do again. And who in Pocahontas is known for stealing other farmers' livestock?"

"Since we were the detectives that caught them, that's easy enough. Those nasty butchers Calvin Cook Senior and Calvin Cook Junior."

Philip was so pleased by my answer that he stopped leaning and jumped up straight as a cotton plant and shook my hand. "I knew that you'd figure it out with a lot of help from me."

"Thanks, Philip, only . . ."

"Only what?"

"Only I hate to tell you this, but the Cooks didn't do it."

"They didn't? You mean they didn't?"

"Nope."

"How come they didn't?"

"Philip, this crime is different. Before, the Cooks stole lots of turkeys with lots of meat that they could sell in their butcher shop to make lots of money. How much meat could you get from sweet, little Baby Beth?"

"Well, you could get *some* meat," he protested. "Maybe a little meat."

"If it were those thieving butchers, they wouldn't have taken off with little Baby Beth. No, they would have stolen her big fat mama, MISS Beth."

Philip made grumbling noises as he went back to his leaning, while I went back to the gate of the pigsty where I continued staring at the wide-as-our-kitchen-door footprint. Without meaning to and without really wanting to, I began talking to myself. "Something ain't right. No, something just ain't right." I kept saying that until finally I was struck by what it was that wasn't right. "Hey! Take off your shoes, Philip, and step into the mud. I want to see your footprints."

"But my feet will get muddy," he whined.

"What *are* you saying?"

"You heard me right the first time."

"Water washes off mud."

"My feet will get cold."

"Oh, and you the bravest of all the brave Tiger Hunters? Them the fellows so brave they ain't feared of nothing? Not even roaring mad tigers?"

"What do you want my footprints for anyway?" he mumbled, while untying his shoes. "You already got his, the Monster of the Mountain's."

"Hurry, Philip, we ain't got all day. You think we've got all day?"

As the top tiger hunter placed one foot and then the other into the chilled scooshy-wooshy ground, he squealed, more like a meek little mouse than a fearless hunter of tigers. For a long moment, I stared at Philip Hall's prints and then stared back at the giant-sized prints. "Look! Well, would you looky there at those foot-prints, Philip! See? See what I see?"

"Yep, sure do," he answered. "That mountain mon-ster's foot is three times bigger than mine."

"Well, yes, but what about the clue? Don't you see the clue?"

He looked a little bit bothered and a little bit more bewildered. "Well, sure, I do. I mean . . . what clue?"

"Philip, look! Look at your footprint. Look at your wrinkled skin lines!"

"Ain't no more wrinkled than anybody else's!" he said, reminding me once again that it doesn't always take a lot to make that sensitive boy mad.

I gave him a few everything-is-okay pats on his back. "As always, you're right! Everybody who has skin has *wrinkled* skin! But now look very closely at the giant footprint and tell me exactly what it is that you *don't* see."

For a time, he examined the super-large footprint and then, for an even longer period of time, he looked back at his own. Finally, he put his nose back within touching distance from the huge foot and smiled. It was a smile that started on one side of his face, but didn't stop until it reached clear across to the other side. "No wrinkles!" he finally blurted out. "My foot has wrinkles. His don't!"

"Spoken like a true detective!" I said, while grabbing his hand in a handshake of victory. "And that means that that wide-as-a-door footprint is nothing but a phony-baloney fake. Maybe somebody wore the fake monster feet over their real feet, you know, like they'd put on a pair of boots."

He scratched his head. "But who . . . who would and why would . . ."

"Because someone wanted to steal Baby Beth, but didn't want to take the blame. The thief wanted the Gorilla Man to take all the blame."

"No!!!!"

"Yes!!!!"

"No, Beth, no!"

"Yes, Philip, YES!!!"

"Now that ain't right!" the top Tiger Hunter blurted out with real feeling. "Ain't nice, either. All those men, all those guns up there on Pinto Mountain."

"We've got to stop them, Philip! And all of them looking to shoot the Monster of the Mountain when he didn't do nothing wrong. Didn't do nobody not even a speck of harm. So we've got to stop them from killing that innocent gorilla guy. But how?"

"Why, we just march up the mountain and tell our people to come on home, 'cause Gorilla Man didn't do it."

This time, it was me leaning against the fence post. "Even if we made it up there, found our men folk, and told them the truth, think they'd believe us?"

My favorite Tiger Hunter slowly and thoughtfully shook his handsome head no. "Don't know. Maybe not. Guess not. Folks around here been hating the Monster of the Mountain for almost forever. They blame him for everything that goes wrong. My daddy blames him when we get too much rain and my mama blames him when we don't get enough rain."

I laughed before remembering how serious this was. "This ain't no laughing matter! We've gotta save the Gorilla Man by finding the real thief and we've gotta save the piglet."

Because the fake monster feet reminded me of the fake monster feet that were sold last Halloween at the Busy Bee, our investigation began at the Busy Bee Bargain Store. Maybe Mr. Putterham might remember some of the people who bought them. The bushy-eyed merchant was leaning over his wrapping counter, so deep in his reading that he didn't see Philip and me until we were right under his lightbulb-shaped nose.

It wasn't until I said, "Howdy, Mr. Putterham," did he look up and lay down the book *Singing Made Easy* on top of another book, which was titled, *Singing Made VERY Easy!*

"Hey, did you kids come in to aggravate me?" he asked. "A poor, hardworking storekeeper with his burdens heavy and his nose stuck to the grindstone! Or did you come in to spend money? One of those things I don't like, but the other one of those things I *do* like. Yep, I like one of those things a whole lot."

"What we are here for, Mr. Putterham, is to investigate the pignapping of Luther's soon-to-be-famous piglet."

From a thick wad of bubble gum, the old Puttydutty

blew a bubble that didn't pop until it struck the point of his nose. "Ha! And Ha again. You crime fighters are too late to fight this crime, 'cause it's already been solved by Sheriff Miller and his rifle-toting men," he said, while picking off the exploded bits of gum that were still sticking to his nose. "Finally, that evil giant will be pumped with more holes that a bakery full of donuts. Boy, oh boy! Serves him right for stealing another man's piglet, 'cause, if you ask me, there's nothing more low down than stealing somebody's sweet little piglet. And that's all I've got to say."

"You said it right well, Mr. Putterham, only I was wondering . . ."

"Yes, girl?"

"I was wondering if you had any more of those fake feet that you sold last Halloween. I sure would like to buy a pair."

The merchant looked surprised. "You actually want to *buy* a pair? What a good girl you are! Everybody needs a pair of fake monster feet, I always say. Did you know I've always said that?"

He led Philip Hall and me into a dark storeroom at the back of the Busy Bee. There he pulled open a large cardboard box marked HALLOWEEN FEET before asking me how many pairs I was buying. When I told him maybe only one pair, when I had the money, he seemed both disappointed and angry. "You're just like them!"

"Just like who?"

"Just like the rest of my customers. You look at the Halloween feet, laugh at them, and call them weird even, but do a single one of you open up your purses? Spend a little money with Pocahontas's leading merchant? Don't you know that I need to sell stuff so I can make money to buy food for my belly?"

"You mean to say, Mr. Putterham, that not a living soul bought a pair of those monster feet?"

"That's what I mean, and ain't that about the saddest thing that you ever did hear? I wanted to sell lots of phony feet, but my stingy customers wouldn't even buy one pair. One pair! Is that too much to ask? Anyway, I don't want to talk about sad things anymore; I want to talk about happy things, like that wicked devil up on Pinto who will soon be dead. Oh, happy, happy days will be here again!"

As the doors of the Busy Bee Bargain Store closed behind Philip and me, I whispered, "Wow! Have you ever got so many clues from just one person? Have we ever done that before?" Just as I got the words out good, I glanced at my crime-fighting partner and I could see that he was looking a little bewildered and a lot bamboozled.

"Uh, you *did* notice all the clues . . . didn't you, Philip?"

"Why . . . why . . . sure! I is a detective, ain't I?"

"Then stop your yapping and let's go to where we're going!"

From the look on his face, I could tell that he had a hundred questions but was too proud to ask a single one of them. I had to find a way to tell him what we were both so busy pretending that he already knew. "So, Philip. I reckon we agree that these are our suspicions that we're both so suspicious about. Number one, the Puttydutty was chewing bubble gum, same as the wrapper found at the pigsty. Number two, since he didn't sell any monster feet, Mr. Putterham is the only person in Pocahontas who already *has* monster feet. Number three, he was reading books on singing, maybe he wanted to have Baby Beth give concerts and make people buy tickets to hear the world's only singing piglet."

"How come you keep telling me what I already be knowing?" said Philip, nasty like, just as though I was wasting his time, and somehow that made me mad. Mad enough to show him up for being what he is: a phony-baloney.

"Okay, Philip, since you already know everything, then why don't you lead the way to where we *are* going?"

"Where we're g-going?" he asked, with just the barest little bit of stuttering in his voice.

"Yes."

"You mean where we're going *now?*"

"Yes."

"Well . . . I knew once, but I think I might have forgot."

"Philip, you don't have to know everything that I know."

"I don't?"

"No, it's not your fault that I'm the smartest girl—the smartest student—in the J. T. Williams School. You don't have to be as smart as me to be special, because you already *are* special. Just the way you are!"

"I am?" he asked, wearing his sweetest and shyest smile.

"You are," I told him. "You positively, definitely are."

The fence that surrounded Mr. Putterham's house was even taller than Philip, and the boards so tight together that there were no cracks wide enough for peeking through. And all along the fence were posted these scary warnings:

B★E★W★A★R★E
Very Hungry
ATTACK DOGS!!!

When I asked Philip Hall to use his long Tiger Hunter legs to jump over and give me a hand up, he shook his head hard while pointing to those signs. "What's the matter with you, Beth Lambert? Can't you read?"

"As good as you," I told him, "only unlike you, I don't believe everything I read. Look, Philip, what is it that dogs do?"

"Dogs do?"

"I mean, what sounds do they make?"

"Bark."

"Right, and do you hear any barking?"

He cupped his hands around his ears before answering, "No."

"And the reason for that is . . . ?"

"But the sign—"

"Forget the sign!"

Taking no chances, Philip filled his pockets with sticks and stones and jumped the fence before dropping down a hands-up to me. And as soon as I struck down on Mr. Putterham's closed-in yard, he said, "Well, you were sure right about the dogs."

"Dogs? What dogs?" I asked quickly glancing this way and that way, as my heart began pumping with alarm.

"Ain't no dogs. What I said was that you were right in thinking that there weren't nary a dog."

"Oh, right, no dogs," I answered, while telling my heart to calm down.

Although I was happy not to see a dog inside the big fenced-in yard, I was unhappy not to see a piglet. But, wait! I thought maybe I heard something. Or maybe it was nothing. Only the nothing that I was hearing sounded as though it was coming from the other side of the yard. But there was nothing there. Nothing except a metal cage that glinted silver in the afternoon sun.

Philip followed at my heels as I ran straight for that cage. All the time, I kept whispering, "Please . . . please let it be her. Let it be her. Let it be—ohh, it is . . . it is BABY BETH! Oh, Baby Beth!" I said, as I slipped back the latch and took her into my arm. "Oh, Baby Beth, it's YOU!"

In the next moment, I had pushed Baby Beth into Philip's surprised arms, telling him to take her back to her mama, Miss Beth, in the pigsty. "We've saved one, and now we've got one more to go! I'm climbing up on Pinto Mountain, 'cause I've got to find the men and tell them that it's not what they think. I've got to tell them, tell the world to leave Gorilla Man alone, 'cause he's an innocent monster, as innocent as a newborn baby."

It wasn't until the second hour of my hunting for the sheriff's posse that I caught sight of all of them up there on the rocky side of the mountain. I began running and stumbling toward them, swinging my arms like a worn-out windmill, while calling Pa's name until finally it happened, first Luther and then Pa and then everybody else saw me too.

At first, they all were all mad at me, especially Sheriff Miller, my own pa, and my brother, 'cause, according to Luther, "I was making enough racket to scare the Monster of the Mountain clear up to the very top of the mountain."

"Well, I really hope so," I told him, told them all. "'Cause the Gorilla guy didn't do it. Mr. Putterham did!"

"No!" the men roared with the voices of many.

"Yes," I answered with the voice of one. "Philip Hall and I found little Baby Beth in his yard, locked up in a cage like a criminal!"

When Sheriff Miller, followed by his rifle-toting men, first began entering the Busy Bee Bargain Store, Mr. Putterham smiled just as though he thought he was gonna sell a lot of deputy sheriffs a lot of stuff. But because the sheriff and his men all looked as though they had eaten bowls of thumbtacks for breakfast, the merchant saw that he wasn't going to be in for much selling or smiling time.

For a long moment, the sheriff glared at the old Puttydutty before the lawman finally got around to asking the first question. "Beth and Phil found the piglet caged inside your fenced yard. Know how Baby Beth got there?"

The storekeeper unwrapped a small block of pink bubble gum and threw it into his mouth. "Same way that the little lamb got to school. It followed Mary. Well, that little piglet of Luther Lambert's did the same exact thing. Followed me home one day, and that's all there is to that!"

When the men's angry-eyed gaze stayed glued to Mr. Putterham, he seemed to understand that his story wasn't believable enough to be believed, so he tried again. "Why,

why, you good men of Pocahontas, surely goodness and mercy, you don't mean to tell me that you think that I—I, Cyrus J. Putterham, the biggest and the best storekeeper in all of Pocahontas, would stoop to stealing livestock. And with such a little bit of a piece of meat at that!"

The sheriff's head bobbed thoughtfully up and then down before telling everybody what he believed. "To tell the truth, Putterham here has a point. 'Cause I can't for the life of me believe that the richest man in town would steal Luther Lambert's piglet, and for what? For such a precious little bit of meat. That don't make no sense, and that's the truth!"

I leaned over the Busy Bee Bargain Store's wrapping counter to raise high the two books lying there, *Singing Made Easy* and *Singing Made VERY Easy!* "Meat ain't the only reason to steal a piglet, 'cause this particular piglet is a genuine singing piglet. Mr. Putterham knows that folks will pay out good money to hear the world's only singing piglet. And Luther here will tell you that she always sings sweetly, although, truth be told, she can't always remember the words. At least not all the words."

Suddenly a shriek filled the air, and it was so frightening that I was sure that it could only come from the mouth of a beast. Only it didn't, it came from the mouth of our piglet-stealing store owner. "*EEEEEEeeeHEAH!!!* That's a lie! A mean and miserable lie! I gave that piglet good food, paid for it out of my own pocket. And how does that piglet show her appreciation? Even Tommy Tucker sang for his supper, which is more than I can say for Baby Beth.

"Why I tried teaching her to sing every morning and I tried teaching her to sing every night, but the only thing that dumb, ole piglet would do was to cry. Cried all day and cried all night. So, little Baby Beth is not only unappreciative, she's also untalented. Didn't sing a single note! No siree bob, not a single, solitary note!"

I shook my head no. "Didn't anyone ever tell you, Mr. Putterham," I asked, "that piglets are a lot like people? They cry when they're sad, but they only sing when they're happy."

7

The Pocahontas Patriot

After school, Mr. Barnes brought the school bus to a squeaky stop at the dusty road leading to our farm. Although I didn't want to seem too anxious to find out what Miss Ramona Thomas had written about us detectives in the paper, I was, just the same, anxious to know what Miss Ramona Thomas had written about us detectives. So, I hugged my books to my chest, did a flying leap off the bus, and ran lickety-split all the way home.

Usually the first thing that I ask Ma is, "What's new?" or "Where's Baby Benjamin?," but this time the only thing I asked was, "Is the paper here?"

"Reckon you want to read all about yourself," said Ma, before nodding toward a copy of the *Pocahontas Weekly News* that was lying on the kitchen table. "And would you looky there at that picture of Luther holding Miss Beth.

Euuu whee! Don't he look handsome?"

"Reckon he sure enough do," I answered, while snatching up the paper. "Almost as handsome as Baby Beth." And there it was staring up at me right on the front page where the most important stories go. I sat down and started to read:

THE POCAHONTAS WEEKLY NEWS
All the news all the time . . .
not just some of the news some of the time!

Luther and Little Pig Together Again
by
Miss Ramona Thomas

Luther Lambert and his talented pig, Baby Beth, are together again, and that is because of the fine detective work by his younger sister, Elizabeth Lorraine Lambert, and her friend Philip Marvin Hall.

Prominent local merchant Mr. Cyrus J. Putterham appeared in court before Judge Elizabeth Bassett for the crime of piglet stealing. But when Mr. Putterham tried to explain that the piglet merely followed him home one day, just like the little lamb that followed Mary to school one day, the judge frowned, saying that she did not believe that he was telling the truth. Judge

Bassett decided that since the pig was such a little pig, the storekeeper was not really guilty of a big crime, only a little crime. So his punishment would not be jail, but something else.

The shaking merchant man was ordered by the black-robed judge to give something big and expensive back to the town. Since the town was going to have an arm-wrestling contest, the judge demanded that Mr. Putterham donate a very important trophy, a winner's belt. Judge Bassett further decided that it should be decorated patriotically with red, white, and blue jewels.

The storekeeper promised the judge that the jeweled belt, which would be known as "The Putterham Prize," would be ready in time for the great arm-wrestling championship, and that it would be mighty beautiful.

"Now ain't that something for the record books," said Ma, reading over my shoulder. "That man who's so stingy that he wouldn't give a person a good word is now gonna give away something for free. Something beautiful. Imagine that!"

"But that's terrible," I told her. "Just terrible. Now even *more* people will be coming into our town just to see the Putterham Prize."

Mama threw her hands against her wide hips as her

expression turned disgusted. "Ain't nothing terrible about folks curious to see something *that* beautiful. How come a girl who was born with more curiosity for a classroom of kindergarteners ain't got no patience for other folks who might have a little curiosity too?"

But before her words were all the way out of her mouth, I was already out the door. Even so, Mama's voice came calling back. But because the wind was doing too much whistling past my ears for me to hear all that my mother said, I walked back into the kitchen. "What was it you were saying," I asked, "something about a barn?"

She glanced up and looked confused. "I didn't say a word about no barn. I said arm, *arm!* Phil has done gone and challenged some poor fellow from Walnut Ridge name of Tyrone Cyclone to an arm-wrestling contest."

"NO!" I told Ma. "Oh, no, he didn't! Well, maybe Philip Hall might have said something like that when he was mad at me, but he's not mad anymore. We're friends now—didn't you know? Didn't I already tell you that?!"

Ma shook her head slowly and sadly. "Beth, honey, you might know what you're talking about, but I sure don't know what you're talking about. But if you want to read all about the arm-wrestling contest, turn to the second page of the paper."

I twirled on my heels, picked up the paper again, and began to read:

81

THE GREAT ARM-WRESTLING CONTEST
by
Miss Ramona Thomas

The great arm-wrestling contest between Pocahontas's own Phil Hall and that other guy, Tyrone the Cyclone, from that other town, Walnut Ridge, will be held at high noon this Saturday in front of the Busy Bee Bargain Store.

The top Tiger Hunter will be defending the honor of all Pocahontians as well as the honor of all Tiger Hunters. The soon-to-be-famous Putterham Prize, a dazzling bejeweled, red-white-and-blue belt will be presented to the winner, naturally enough, our guy. The prize was donated by the merchant Cyrus J. Putterham, who used to be stingy but is now generous.

Pocahontas mayor, Benjamin Potter, has sent this arm-wrestling challenge to Mayor Ernie O'Connor of Walnut Ridge. "If Tyrone ain't too scared to show up for the wrestling, then let him show up. But if he's too scared, then send somebody who might be a little braver. HA! And Ha again!!!"

The more I read, the more I understood that if I only do one thing in my life, I had to stop the arm-wrestling contest before everybody found out that there ain't no

Cyclone. Ain't even no Tyrone! Somebody had to call off the contest, and there was only one person in all this world that could do that.

I raced out of our house like my fanny was on fire, and I didn't even once slow down until I skidded to a stop in front of Mr. Nathaniel Hall's fancy new dairy barn. As soon as I stepped through the door, I saw that whatever was going on, it was sure enough strange stuff. The old Puttydutty himself was measuring the length of Philip's right arm, while Sheriff Nathan Miller was giving him strength training for his left arm.

Although Philip Hall managed to glance at me, he was too busy getting measured up and muscled up to do anything more than quickly nod in my direction. So I quietly asked, "Well, what's happening, Philip?"

"What's happening? You mean you don't know what's happening?" sputtered Mr. Cyrus J. Putterham while pitty-patting Philip on the shoulder. "Why, this here young Pocahontas Patriot is going to defend the honor of all Pocahontians, all Tiger Hunters, and he is going to do it while wearing the glittering, gold, muscle-man costume that advertises the finest store in all of Pocahontas. My store, the Busy Bee Bargain Store! And now you know, you nosey detective, you!"

Philip frowned at Mr. Putterham, and I thought for sure that he was going to tell the storekeeper to talk polite to the best friend he has in all the world, but I was wrong.

He only began complaining about his costume. "You told me that the costume was going to say CHAMPION PHIL HALL."

"Ohh, it's going to say CHAMPION PHIL HALL alright, only in tiny, little letters on the front," Mr. Putterham answered. "But the back of the costume, in great glittering letters, it's going to say THE BUSY BEE BARGAIN STORE."

"Uhh, Philip," I said, breaking in when I knew that nobody wanted me to go breaking in. "We've *got* to talk."

Both Sheriff Miller and Mr. Putterham gave me a look that wasn't what you'd call friendly.

"So, go right ahead and talk, Beth," said Philip pleasantly. "My arm might be busy, but my ears ain't. So you just go ahead and talk away."

"In private, Philip! In *private!*"

The sheriff tugged at the storekeeper's arm, pulling him away from his measuring, while calling back over his shoulder to me, "Okay, Beth, but don't make a day of it. Phil has his arm-wrestling training, his costume measurements, and Miss Ramona Thomas is outside waiting to take a picture of Pocahontas's finest! Our soon-to-be arm-wrestling champion!"

Philip Hall turned his beaming-with-pleasure-and-pride face toward me. "Ain't I something else? I'm gonna have my picture in the paper and my very own wrestling costume. People as far away as Jonesboro, Pine Bluff, Wynne, and Hot Springs and Eureka Springs, too, is gonna know my name. Gonna know me, Phil Hall, the great arm-wrestling champion from good ole Pocahontas, Arkansas, U.S.A.!"

"You ought not go counting your arm-wrestling championships before you win one."

"Well, I'm gonna win one on Saturday. You'll see!"

"Stop it, Philip! STOP IT!!! You can't be the champ, 'cause I only said what I said about Tyrone the Cyclone back when we were mad, but we ain't mad. Not anymore. We're friends now. Remember, we're FRIENDS!"

He smiled his cutest little dimpled smile. "Oh, I reckon I already know that, 'cause without you, I might not have solved the mystery of the missing piglet quick as I did."

I just about reminded that boy that I did a lot more than just *help* him solve the mystery. Looks like he plum forgot that I was a full and equal partner, and while I thought about telling him what I thought . . . I thought I shouldn't. Getting him mad at me now is the last thing I need. "Uhh, Philip, uhh . . . can you remember back how we got so rip-roaring mad at each other? You know, when I first came back home from Walnut Ridge?"

Suddenly, he was shaking a finger in my direction. "You think I go around holding grudges for something that you said but shouldn't have said weeks ago? Nah, I forgive you for all those dumb-stupid things you said."

"I didn't just say something dumb . . . I also said . . ."

"What?"

"I also . . . well . . ."

"Well, what?"

"I also told you what wasn't true."

His forehead wrinkled. "You mean—you don't mean a lie?"

I nodded yes, and when I did that he showed his interest by jutting his neck forward. Now we were nose-to-nose. "Well, what did you lie about, Beth?"

From the corner of my eye, I saw that both the sheriff and the storekeeper were quickly walking back and I knew I had to talk fast. "What I lied about was Tyrone the Cyclone, 'cause he ain't what I told you he was, 'cause, the fact is, he ain't never been nobody, 'cause he's nothing. He's nobody at all!"

Suddenly he slapped his thigh before grinning like he had already won ten thousand arm-wrestling championships. "Detective that I am, I reckon that I already knew that, 'cause what you were doing was trying to make me jealous. Now ain't that the Bible truth?"

My head did little bounces up and then even little bounces down. Up and then down. "Well, I guess I . . . yes, I guess I . . ."

Then Sheriff Miller's powerful voice called across the barn, "Okay, Beth, now get a move on. We men folk got us important work to do."

I grabbed Philip's hand. "Now you know that you can't go fighting nothing, 'cause nothing ain't never gonna be nothing but nothing. Now do you understand?"

For the smallest sliver of a moment, Philip Hall looked as puzzled as if he had just been trying to understand the babblings of babies. And that's when Sheriff Miller touched my elbow while gesturing toward the barn door.

Following the orders of our lawman, I took a couple of steps away before turning back toward Philip. "So tell them what I already done told you. That there's nothing to arm wrestle with, okay, Philip?"

Philip Hall didn't answer, probably because he was too busy being measured up and muscled up. But just the same, I'm sure he heard me because I saw him smile, so I know he understood. At least, I reckon maybe.

8

Beth's Bad Luck, Terrible Day

On the school bus the next morning, all the Pretty Pennies (excepting Bonnie) finally started acting friendly to me once again. Well, maybe they weren't so much friendly as they were desperate.

"So, you just gotta help us," explained the gorgeous one, nodding toward the front of the bus where a heads-down Bonnie was writing furiously on lined paper. "'Cause she won't let us have our Swing-Your-Partner Dance until she finishes writing up her rules."

Esther moaned. "And we're all gonna be old ladies long before that happens!"

"Oh, it couldn't be as bad as all that," I said, while standing up and jutting my head forward. If only I could make out what Bonnie is writing, I could prove to them all that she's probably, right this very minute, making secret plans for our almost-famous Swing-Your-Partner party. With my stretched and bent neck, I was able to make out what she had written, but the only thing there were these three words written in bold, black letters: RULE NUMBER **283.**

The next thing I knew I had given my solemn Pretty Penny promise to Ginny, Esther, and Susan that I'd talk to Bonnie about our every-year dance. And that I'd talk to her right *now*, right this minute.

"Howdy, Bonnie," I said, swinging into the bus seat next to her.

She glanced up at me just as though I was some sneaky snake in the grass slithering myself ever closer her way. "We Pretty Pennies *already* have a president," she announced, while tapping on her own chest just so I'd know exactly which president she was talking about.

"Reckon you don't have to tell me what I already know!" For a while neither she nor I said a word, and then finally I did. "Well, what are you doing, Bonnie?"

She sighed as though talking with someone as dumb as me took an awful lot of patience. "Right now I'm hard at work on the mustard rules."

"The . . . the mustard rules?"

"Are you hard of hearing? That's what I said, the *mustard* rules."

"Well, why? I mean how come we *need* mustard rules?"

"'Cause we might someday eat hot dogs again like we did before. Remember when we grilled hot dogs down on the banks of the Black River?"

"Well, yeah, Bonnie, but that was a long time ago. . . ."

"But if we *ever* do it again, we'll do it right this time, with rules. Not like we did it before, with some girls slapping their mustard on one side of the buns and other girls slapping the mustard on the other side of the bun."

"But what's wrong with that?"

"Doesn't surprise me one little bit, Beth Lambert, that you see nothing wrong with that, even though what you did was the worst. And that's why we gotta have more rules, so that nobody ever again does that terrible thing that you done did wrong."

I tried remembering what I couldn't seem to remember. "I mean, what was it that I did do? Do wrong?"

"What you did wrong?" Bonnie repeated, just as though I had asked the world's dumbest question. "Mustarding the right side of the bun wasn't good enough for you. Mustarding the left side of the bun wasn't good enough for you. So what did you do? You went and done something else!"

Although I couldn't exactly remember what it was that I did do way back then, I could tell by the fury in her voice that it must have been bad. Really bad! So bad that I was a little afraid to come right out and ask, but even so, I finally did. "Well, what was it that I did do, Bonnie?"

"What you did was the very thing that you should never have done! All the other Pennies slapped their mustard on the right side of their bun or on the left side of their bun, but that's not what you did!"

"It's not?"

"No, you globbed your mustard right on top of your hot dog, and so that, Beth Lambert, is what you did!"

Because Mr. Barnes had turned into the school's parking lot, I could tell that there was no more time for any more mustard talk. I had to get down to the serious business of asking the new president in one big hurry about what Pennies were so desperate to know.

"Uh, well, Bonnie, the girls want to know about our Swing-Your-Partner Dance. They want to know if you're making plans."

My question surprised her so much that she looked as though somebody had slapped her hard across her face.

She slammed down a notebook labeled THE RULES AND REGULATIONS AND LAWS OF BONNIE BLAKE (THE PRECIOUS NEW PRESIDENT OF THE PRETTY PENNY CLUB OF POCAHONTAS, ARKANSAS). "How can I even think about unimportant stuff like our Swing-Your-Partner Dance," she asked, "when I've still got a lot more rules waiting to be written?"

We kids hadn't hopped off the school bus good when two really silly girls from Miss Ursula Willis's homeroom began jumping up and down like croaking toads all around Philip Hall, begging to feel his arm-wrestling muscles. I didn't hang around long enough to see how embarrassed he must have been. Anyway, I was feeling sorrier and sorrier about who'd have to explain that there ain't gonna be no arm wrestling, 'cause there ain't no Tyrone the Cyclone.

As soon as I walked into my homeroom, I saw Miss Johnson carefully chalking these words on the blackboard: *2nd Period—ASSEMBLY.*

"What's the assembly about, Miss Johnson?"

She looked puzzled. "Don't rightly know, Beth. We teachers are always given plenty of advance notice before our assemblies, but not this time. Must sure be important."

As soon as the second-period bell rang, a thundering herd of feet began stomping into the auditorium, 'cause every student always wants the very same thing: a seat as close to the stage as possible. But this time, I was really lucky. First row and smack dab in the middle. WOW! Was this my lucky day . . . or what?

We weren't what you'd call all settled down good when that familiar little man with the big belly strode across the stage like he owned the place. As he stood on his tippy tiptoes trying hard to reach the standing microphone, some kids were rude enough to giggle. Reckon I giggled too. I didn't mean to be rude, but I know that I was.

Finally reaching the microphone, he bellowed out,

"Howdy, boys and girls."

In unison, we all called back, "Howdy, Mayor Potter."

"You are all probably wondering why I'm here today," said the boss of Pocahontas. "Well, I'm gonna tell you why I'm here, 'cause I'm as proud as a peacock to be here. Oh, *Diddly Wah DODODO!* 'Cause on Saturday, in front of the Busy Bee Bargain Store, the great arm-wrestling championship is gonna take place. And after nine long years of losing to Walnut Ridge in basketball, baseball, and football, we Pocahontians are finally gonna do some winning on our own! Ohh, yes siree, we are going to win the arm-wrestling championship!!!"

As the great room began cheering the mayor's words, I looked around for Philip Hall, knowing that he would be shaking his head long and hard in Mayor Potter's direction so that he and everybody else would understand that there's been a bad mistake. But amid a sea of faces, I couldn't find his, the one face that would tell us all that there will be no arm-wrestling contest. No winner and no loser.

But the only face I saw was the mayor's. "I, the great mayor of the greatest little town in Arkansas, make this promise: this time, we're gonna win! And for the glory and honor of Pocahontas, we want you all—each and every one of you—to come cheer our very own Phil Hall against that weak-kneed little weakling from Walnut Ridge. 'Cause we all know that Cyclone Tyrone ain't much, and neither is his town, his Walnut Ridge! And that's the truth!"

I tried to get Mayor Potter's attention, tried to show him by my hand motions that the arm-wrestling contest had been called off, but he went right on talking. Mostly about how the Walnut Ridge High School football team, year after year after year, does the same terrible thing. They beat the Pocahontas High School football team. "And the really rotten thing about that," he said, while shaking a pudgy finger at us all, "is that our football team is a lot better than their football team. And if you don't believe me, then just ask anybody here in Pocahontas. They'll tell you!"

Everybody was clapping and whistling so hard that the mayor had to stop his talking and settle for merely waving. "And now," he continued, "without any more falderal or falderoo, I'm going to ask the one fellow who's gonna hand us that oh-so-sweet victory to say a few words. Phil Hall, trot yourself on up here!"

And there he came, striding briskly up on the stage, looking for the world as though he had already won a hundred arm-wrestling contests. Then it broke out. From all over the auditorium, it broke out. And now every voice was singing out: "Two, four, six, eight—Who do we ap-pre-ci-ate? Phil—YEA! Hall—YEA! PHIL HALL—YEA!!! YEA!!! YEA!!!"

As Philip Hall stood straight and tall before the mike,

like the king of the world, not saying a word, only waiting till all the cheering stopped, I felt real sorry for him.
I mean, it won't be one bit easy for him to tell folks what
they'd never want to hear. Especially since everybody in
this auditorium thinks he's gonna say one thing, when I
(and only I) know that he's gonna say another thing.

"All I want to say," said Philip Hall, rubbing his hands
together just as though he could hardly wait for the arm
wrestling to begin, "is that I sure do want to thank Mayor
Potter for sending that invitation to Tyrone the Cyclone
or any brave soul from Walnut Ridge who is dumb
enough to wrestle me.

"And I thank Sheriff Miller, who gave me the best arm-
wrestling training any boy could have, and also Miss
Ramona Thomas, who took my picture for the newspaper.
Mr. Putterham I want to thank, too, for finally doing the
right thing and giving me my arm-wrestling costume, and
come Saturday, he'll be giving me the best thing of all: the
Putterham Prize."

What, I wondered, was that boy saying? Did even he
know what he was saying? Just then, Mayor Potter again
rose to his tippy toes before pushing his face against the
mike. "Phil, why don't you tell everybody what I'm gonna
do if Tyrone the Cyclone tries to chicken out and he can't
get anybody else either brave enough or foolish enough to
wrestle in his place? Tell everybody that they're still gonna
lose the contest. They'll lose by default."

Not until I saw Philip Hall edge himself in front of the mayor did I begin to understand how much that boy loves being in the center of everybody's eyes. "And what I'm gonna do," said the top Tiger Hunter, "is tell that poor, pathetic Walnutter that if he's too weak . . . or even too scared to face up to me in arm-to-arm wrestling, then he can send in his big brother—or any one of them nutty Walnutters. I'll take any one of them folks on! Why, I might even take them all on!"

Then, from all across assembly, there were voices followed by clapping and whistling. That's when they began cheering Philip Hall's fiercely fighting words: "Rrrr-ooolll Tyrone Cyclone O-ver, and lay him flat, Flat, FLAT! Pin that Wal-nutter's arm to the mat, Mat, MAT!"

Suddenly, the auditorium was ringing with cheers, claps, and fierce foot stompings. I couldn't think of anywhere in this world that I wanted to be. I only knew that this was the one place that I couldn't be. So, I jumped out of my seat and raced through the room and out the door.

On Saturday, Pa took a left turn off the highway to drive into downtown Pocahontas. Although Annie and Luther jumped up in the cargo area of the truck to better see what kind of excitement there would be on this champion arm-wrestling day, I stayed curled up in the corner like a cat napping.

"Come on, let's go," Annie said, while giving my arm a tug.

"No need to go getting yourself all worked up about nothing," I warned. "'Cause what's gonna happen today ain't gonna amount to a hill of beans."

Annie bent low over me giving me a long, hard look. "How come you is so down on this day, eh, baby sister? Is it 'cause this is the only Pocahontas fun day that wasn't planned by you?"

I shook my head. "No, that's not it."

"Well, is it because you're a little jealous, 'cause this time, for the first time, everybody is talking about Phil? And nobody is talking about you?"

Again I shook my head no, because I didn't want anybody talking about me. And I was afraid that before this very day was over, everybody would be talking about me. Only what they'd be saying wouldn't be very nice.

Annie looked at me long and hard before asking, "Then how come you look all weary and weighted down with worry?"

"'Cause a secret can be a mighty heavy thing to carry," I told her. "Especially when you have to carry it alone."

Annie suddenly pointed to a great sign that was strung across Main Street. "Well, Lordy! Lordy!" she screeched. "Would you looky there!"

Although the oversized sign kept fluttering this way and that way in the breezy breeze, I was still able to read:

COME ONE! COME ALL! SEE PHIL HALL BEAT THE NUTTY
WAL-NUTTER POOR LITTLE SWEET LITTLE CYCLONE
TYRONE OHH . . . PLEASE . . . DON'T YOU CRY OHH . . .
PLEASE . . . DON'T YOU MOAN 'CAUSE THE DOCTORS AND
NURSES HAVE ALL BEEN PHONED!

As I read the sign, I groaned. But then I figured things couldn't be as bad as I thought, so I read it again. Only this time, I knew that things were even worse than I thought. So, I groaned again, only this time louder.

Annie was shaking my arm. "What's the matter with you, Beth? Is you hurting?"

"No," I answered at the same time I thought silently to myself, I'm not hurting half as much as I will be when folks find out that I'm nothing but a lying phony.

As Pa turned and angle parked his truck in front of the Busy Bee Bargain Store, Annie was again pulling on my arm. "Come on, come on, Beth, get off the truck. Watching all these exciting goings-on is gonna help you out a whole heap."

Because of Annie's nonstop urgings, I obediently jumped off the back of the parked truck. Even so, it's going to take more than exciting goings-on to make me feel better, 'cause if it weren't for these "goings-on," I would already be feeling better. Fact is, I'm not expecting to feel any better, not today, not tomorrow, and maybe not ever.

9

The Great Arm-Wrestling Contest

As my fancy Annie of a sister pulled me along Pocahontas's thick-with-people Main Street, it reminded me of last summer's Old Rugged Cross Church picnic. Oh, not so much the picnic as the picnic table, where armies of ants fought to their deaths over a few yellowy crumbs of sugary Twinkies. At any rate, I'm sure I've never before seen so many ants then and I've never seen so many people now.

Annie tugged at my sleeve before pointing to the platform in front of the Busy Bee Bargain Store, where two empty chairs sat across a sturdy table. "Hey! Would you take a gander at that arm-wrestling platform? So fresh and new you can still smell the pine boards. Looks like the old Puttydutty didn't spare any expense. Got to give him credit; he sure did things up right!"

"Well, no credit to him. The judge herself told the Puttydutty that if he had spared the expense, he wouldn't have been spared jail time."

And although there wasn't anything to see excepting that perfectly ordinary table and those even more ordinary chairs, men with children riding on their shoulders and women with babies in their arms were squirming this a-way and that a-way and every which a-way to worm their way still closer to the now-empty wrestling platform.

Everybody was just babbling and bouncing over with excitement. Happy and excited that something was going to happen—that very soon now, everybody knew, something very big was just about to happen right up there on that platform.

We eased ourselves around Cold Soda Sam's wheeled food cart heavy with his corndogs and even more famous eat-'em-while-they're-hot chilidogs. Hereabouts boys aren't considered men until they're able to gobble down at least two without catching their insides on fire. But on second thought, it didn't much matter how hot the fire rages inside your body as long as you can keep the pain from showing up on your face.

All up and down Main Street, folks talked happily and excitedly about how Phil Hall was finally going to bring all the lost honor and glory back to Pocahontas. Especially all the honor and glory that we Pocahontians lost to Walnut Ridge during those nine terrible, awful years of lost football, basketball, and baseball games.

One white-haired woman latching both her hands firmly onto her hips explained her views to a friend who was even more white haired than she. "What suits my fancy is that all them stuck-up folks over there in Walnut Ridge is gonna finally learn how it feels to lose."

"Well, what would you expect from those people?" her friend replied. "If you ask me, folks who name their town after a nut has got to be more than a little nutty."

"Hey, the cheerleaders! Looky!" cried Annie. "All six of them are here to cheer Phil Hall onto victory. And don't they look fine in their cute little whirly and twirly costumes?"

I shook my head no. "To tell the truth, I think they look dumb."

Annie turned fast to check me out eyeball to eyeball. "You sure enough look like the Beth Lambert that I've known all my born days, but you sure don't act like the Beth Lambert that I've known all my born days."

But since the parade down Main Street of the John Deere tractors had just begun, my sister's interest in me, thankfully, became less and her interest in those slow-driving tractor drivers became more. Seemed like the slower they drove, the more red-and-white striped candy canes they'd throw out to the excited crowd.

Following the latest display of John Deere farm

equipment were the marching members of the Pocahontas Volunteer Fire Department, all booted and yellow suited. Across their shoulders, they carried their fire axes the same way marching soldiers carry their rifles.

It wouldn't take a person but one look to tell that there ain't no better firemen anywhere than our fearless firemen of Pocahontas, Arkansas. And just behind our firefighters was our gleaming red fire truck polished so brightly that its sides reflected, like a shiny mirror, all the faces in the crowd.

Farther down Main Street, Annie and I stopped at this sidewalk table with the big sign:

OLD RUGGED CROSS CHURCH WOMEN'S AUXILIARY— GOOD EATS. "NOURISHMENT FOR YOUR SOUL . . . AND YOUR BELLY." (ALL MONIES GO TO THE OLD RUGGED CROSS BUILDING FUND)

My mama and Mrs. Ross, the preacher's wife, were so busy serving up plates heavy with fried turkey, mustard greens, and topped with a large slab of golden brown cornbread that it was clear that they didn't have no time for no conversing. Just the same, as Annie and I started to move away, Mama held at eye level the glass jar heavy with money from their sold food before giving it a dramatic rattle in my direction. "Our building fund is doing fine, girls," she told us. "Real fine."

"Oh, that's good, Mama," I answered, but I wondered

if she could tell just by the dull sound of my voice that my heart wasn't really into anything but crying. Yeah, crying, that was something that I could easily do.

Then from a distance, we heard the Pocahontas High School marching band strike up their musical tribute to Philip Hall called, "For He's a Jolly Good Fellow." The band probably thought that that would make Philip all raring to go, but I know different. Probably I'm the only one in the whole wide world that knows this, and I've known it for so long that it doesn't even seem like a secret anymore. Reckon it just seems . . . well, natural, like just the way things are, and always have been.

Anyway, if it's still a secret, I sure hope that nobody goes around tattling to others, but the truth is that of all Philip's wonderful qualities, bravery just ain't one of them. Oh, I know he's called the bravest Tiger Hunter of them all, but there's a reason for that. And if people ever got around to thinking about it, then they could figure out the *real* reason for themselves. At any rate, don't expect me to be the one who squeals!

And not being brave, and not wanting anybody to know it, Philip Hall is, at this very moment, probably as nervous as a cat who is about to lose his ninth life. Problem is that there had been lies, and then when I tried to straighten out the lie, I made this even stupider mistake. When I tried to explain to Philip, for example, that Tyrone the Cyclone was not real, I made the mistake of saying he was "nothing." And the more I thought about it, the more I came to understand that Philip took that wrong. He took that to mean that Tyrone was some little pathetic somebody who ain't worth worrying about because he ain't got no arm-wrestling muscles worth nothing.

But now Philip Hall sees that the stage is set and folks from all around have come flooding into Pocahontas a lot like the way the flood water flushed through our town way back when the dam broke. And like the water that washed through Pocahontas, I know he's scared to death of being washed away by a bigger, stronger opponent. And could the people of Pocahontas really stand losing? Could Philip Hall?

Oh, in my mind's eye, I can picture Philip now, all sweaty and nervous. Pacing this a-way and then pacing that a-way. Asking himself how he got into this mess. Asking himself how he could (without anybody calling him chicken) chicken out.

All at once, the microphone-amplified voice of Mayor Potter was heard over all the other voices. "Ladies and Gentlemen, let's all give a great, big welcoming hand to our wonderful Pocahontas High School cheerleaders, who have come here today to cheer the Pocahontas Patriot on to victory!"

Suddenly, everybody was clapping and cheering. Even folks who were holding onto their corndogs and chilidogs quickly stuck them into their mouths so that their hands would be free to clap, clap, and then CLAP some more.

Then the cheerleaders raced out of the Busy Bee Bargain Store and up onto the platform, while shouting for victory from the very top of their lungs: "On to Vic-tory! On to Vic-tory! Fight! Fight! Fight! Fight! Fight! For the Glo-ry of Our Hero in Gold—a Win Win WIN Is Our Goal! Sooo . . . It's on to Vic-tory! On to Vic-tory! On to VIC-TOR-Y! Fight! Fight! Fight! PHIL HALL! FIGHT!!!"

Then nobody but Mr. Cyrus J. Putterham himself, arms waving, marched proudly into the wrestler's ring, carrying his sparkle-a-plenty belt dazzling with red, white, and blue jewels. "What I got here," he explained, "is the great arm-wrestling championship belt that I and I alone paid for out of the goodness and generosity of my kind heart."

Then a voice from the crowd—sounded a lot like Bubba Wilson's voice—hollered back. "Oh, come on now, Putterham! A lot of us folks have trouble believing that you've got any heart at all, leastways not a kind and generous one."

Some people laughed and a couple of people even impolitely recalled that Mr. Putterham's gift might have a lot more to do with staying out of jail than with being good and generous. Even so, the old Puttydutty just flicked off those annoying words like he might flick off a few pesky flies at a barbecue, as he went right on talking.

"What I got here is the great arm-wrestling championship belt, which is going to be worn by—," he winked slyly at the listening crowd. "Well . . . I reckon we all know what fellow is going to win this here belt today, now don't we?"

Some folks clapped and some folks whistled and some folks even managed to do both. The really disgusting thing, though, were those same girls from Miss Ursula Willis's homeroom class. They were screaming and pulling on their hair just like Philip Hall was a Country-and-Western singing star or something. Oh, please!

Even so, the storekeeper went right on talking, while pointing toward the door of his store. "So, without any more falderal or folderol, I take pleasure and I take pride in introducing somebody that you all already know."

From the crowd, a man's voice (this time I knew for sure it was nobody else's but Mr. Bubba Wilson's) rang out, "Come on, Putterham, get on with it, will you? We didn't come to hear you yip, yap, and flap your tongue. Besides, nobody here needs you to introduce Phil Hall, 'cause we've all been knowing him since he was knee high to a bumblebee."

"Okay! Okay!" said Mr. Putterham. "Come on, all you loyal Pocahontians, applaud till your hands fall off! Applaud for our guy, Phil Hall, the Pocahontas Patriot!"

While the folks cheered for Philip Hall, I was, for the first time in my life, feeling sorry for the old Puttydutty.

'Cause he's going to be looking pretty foolish introducing Philip Hall, who ain't nowhere to be seen. One thing I was sure about was that the top Tiger Hunter had already done what I already knew he'd do: chicken out.

And that's when I saw them marching Tiger Hunters proudly tapping out rhythms with their sticks on old Maxwell House coffee cans. Two tin-can-beating Tiger Hunters marching in front, and two tin-can-beating Tiger Hunters marching in back. And there, walking tall, right there in the center, like a great dressed-in-gold hero, was . . . Philip Hall!

After a while, even the thundering applause for the Pocahontas Patriot stopped thundering, and that's when folks began to notice that something was wrong or, at least, missing. Soon they were asking, "Well, where is he? That other guy? And how can there be a contest without contestants? *Two* contestants?"

And, like before, Mister Bubba Wilson began yelling out ridicule, only this time his target was different. Now the reason for his anger was no longer the present and prompt Puttydutty, but the very absent and very much missed Tyrone the Cyclone. "That Tyrone ain't no cyclone! If you ask me, he ain't nothing but a little ball of gathering dust."

That's when Suby Sue jumped up straight into the air with pretty poetry of her very own. "Tyrone's ain't no cyclone 'cause he's scared all the way down to the bone!"

107

As folks kept busy making Walnut Ridge and Cyclone jokes with their tongues, their necks were busy craning west toward Walnut Ridge. Every so often somebody would shriek out something about the sound of a vehicle heading down the Walnut Ridge road toward us, but it never turned out to be the right vehicle or, at least, the vehicle carrying Tyrone the Cyclone.

After a while, the jokes got fewer and fewer and the Arkansas sun got brighter and brighter, and hotter and hotter. Beneath every straw hat, rivulets of sweat rolled like miniature mountain streams, and still the one person who folks waited for and prayed for didn't show.

I kept looking for signs, hoping against hope that people would weary and wander off, but although everybody was sure enough weary, not one single soul wandered off. I said to myself, *I'm the only one here that could make folks understand. Could make them go off in search of a bit of a breeze or even a sliver of shade. If only I had half the courage of a goose, I'd stride up there on that there wrestler's ring and talk to the people. Tell them what they need to know: the truth! Yeah, if only I had a tiny cup of courage, that's exactly what I'd do!*

Even as I stood there, talking to myself, telling myself how ashamed I was for not speaking up, for not speaking the truth, I heard the scream. And that's when I saw her—Suby Sue's nearly grown daughter Bonavita waving her arms while screeching for help. Everybody was hollering, everybody was trying to help poor Suby Sue whose knees had knuckled under her before fainting away.

In the next moments, though, Suby Sue herself was jumping up and down while waving greetings to all those who were concerned about her health. All that waving told us that, well, yes, she may have gotten a little overheated, but still and all she was just fine and as dandy as candy.

That's when I understood that I didn't have any choice in this world but to do what I had to do: the right thing. The next time somebody fell away in the heat, we might not be so lucky. So, no matter how much folks would hate me when I fessed up to the terrible truth, I had to do *what I had to do*. And I had to do it NOW!

10

The Piglet-sized Lie that Grew and Grew and G*R*E*W!!!

As I bolted up the single step to the wrestling platform, I suddenly saw flashes of mad across Philip Hall's face. "You ain't supposed to be up here, girl," he hollered. "This place is only for us . . . us brave arm wrestlers!"

Although I heard him, I pretended that I didn't. There were more important things needed saying, and there were many more people I needed saying it to.

Looking down at all those faces that I grew up knowing, I wondered if there was a good way to tell them about the bad stuff that needed telling. For this moment, these seconds before the telling, I knew that (with the exception of the Pretty Pennies) I had a whole town full of friends. But what about afterward? What about all those moments and minutes, hours and years afterward?

Afterward, would I still have a friend, even one friend, to call my very own?

Even though I didn't know what I was going to say or how I was going to say it, I saw myself doing what Miss Johnson always does when she wants quiet in the classroom: she raises her right hand. And, the truth is, all these folks waiting under the harsh heat of the day weren't nearly as obedient as we students of Miss Johnson. 'Cause what the onlookers did was to begin calling back, "We want Tyrone the Cyclone! We want Tyrone the Cyclone!"

Somehow, though, I was able to shout out over their hollering, "That's what I want to talk to you all about."

"We want Tyrone the Cyclone!" But the people wouldn't, not for a moment, stop their chanting, just like I wasn't standing here trying my best to explain. "We WANT Tyrone the Cyclone!"

Again, I raised my hand, actually hands, *both* hands. And what didn't work before seemed to be working pretty good now, 'cause everybody had hushed themselves down. Hushed down real good, 'cause now it was so quiet that I could hear the wind making strange whistling noises in the distance. But now wasn't the right time to think about windy weather, 'cause a hundred faces were looking up at me, looking for answers, and so I began to talk.

"What happened was my fault, all my fault, so don't for a minute think it was Philip Hall's fault 'cause—"

Our school-bus driver, Mr. Barnes, interrupted,

"Don't rightly know what you're talking about, Beth, so why don't you just tell us what we want to know? Is that cyclone fellow coming out or not?"

"Or is he in hiding like I suspect," boomed out Sheriff Miller. "Like some stinking skunk stuck inside a sewer hole?"

"Uh, well, no sir, he ain't exactly doing that either, 'cause, you see, what happened was that Philip Hall and I had this argument so . . . so you see . . . I told a piglet-sized lie, not knowing—not even remembering that little piglets grows up to be Miss Beth–sized hogs, and piglet-sized lies grow up to be—"

This time is was Miz Suby Sue Wallace who stopped me from talking by calling out, "Don't go beating on yourself about fussing with your boyfriend, Beth. Fussing between men folk and women folk—why, that ain't never gonna change. Ain't changed since Mrs. Noah fussed with Mr. Noah about all them strange creatures with muddy hoofs dirtying up her nice, clean ark."

Here and there I heard a splattering of giggles, chuckles, and at least a couple of big, booming belly laughs, thanks to Miz Suby Sue's funny words. But I also heard something else: the whistle of the wind on this hot, still day was whistling still louder. But could that really be? Isn't it the wind that teaches the air how to whistle?

But after more listening, it didn't so much sound like the wind as it did . . . but, no, it couldn't be. That wouldn't make any sense at all!

All heads were now doing exactly the same thing that my head was doing. Gawking and gazing off in the direction of the strange sounds, in the direction of Walnut Ridge!

Our school-bus driver cupped his hand around his ears before calling out, "Well . . . I'll be a monkey's uncle if it ain't the Walnut Ridge Police, and they're heading this way!"

Sheriff Miller corrected. "As old as you are, Barnes, you oughta hear the difference between police sirens and *fire* sirens! Any fool can tell you that what we're hearing is a firetruck. Firetruck sirens!"

At first, folks began craning their necks here, there, and everywhere for the sight of a fire and sniffing the air for a puff of smoke. But there was nothing to smell and nothing to see. No, not even a puff of a cloud!

The next thing that people were saying was that since there was no fire, then he just had to be on that firetruck, Tyrone the Cyclone did. That's when people began shoving and pushing to get closer still to the wrestling ring. Folks were now crammed so close together that there wasn't room for anything else between them, no, not even a piece of tissue paper.

With each moment that ticked on by, the sirens seemed to be more shrilly screaming, and then it happened! The siren-blowing, bell-clanging fire engine with the big, bold, gold lettering, WALNUT RIDGE FIRE DEPT., came to an ear-jarring screech of a stop within a hop of the wrestling ring!

And when folks saw the skinny, old woman driver, their eyes almost came popping out of their heads. Reckon I was surprised too, 'cause the driver was one of the people that I love best in all the world. It was my own Mama Regina!

Although nobody was paying much attention to my grandmother, folks were sure enough pressing against and paying attention to the great fire engine. Poking under the fire hoses while checking under and through the wooden ladders. All the while saying things like, "Maybe that Cyclone fellow is hiding under those hoses or maybe above the ladders."

All at once, Mama Regina cupped her hands around her mouth before calling out, "What's the matter with you Pocahontas ninnies? Sticking your noses into my firetruck? Ain't none of you ever seen a firetruck before? A firetruck painted red?"

Following my grandmother's words, there was a sudden gasp that sounded like a hundred people had all been kicked in the stomach by the same mule and all at the exact, same moment. Sticking his jaw up and out, Sheriff Nathan Miller strode directly over to face my grandmother. "Ma'am, we Pocahontians have always been taught to respect our elders, especially when they is as old and weak as you. So, even though you've insulted us all by calling us ninnies, we are still going to allow you to leave peacefully, letting no harm come to you. So, good-bye!"

She shook her stubborn head. "I ain't fixing to leave till you hand over that pretty Putterham prize!" demanded Mama Regina. "'Cause on this very day, I'm going to be wearing that fancy dancy belt with my do-si-do skirt, 'cause, you see, folks, tonight I'm square dancing."

The sheriff put his hand over his mouth to hide his smirky smile. "Ma'am, let me see if I can make you understand. The Putterham Prize ain't what you think it is. Not just some nice, little present we give people on their birthday, nothing like that. It's a prize given to the winner of our championship arm-wrestling contest between Phil Hall and Tyrone the Cyclone. Only, your Cyclone, knowing he couldn't win, didn't even have the courage to show up. And that's the truth!"

Pulling a folded copy of the *Pocahontas News* out of her flowery apron pocket, Mama Regina read with a voice loud enough and squeaky enough for all to hear: "And so I, Mayor Potter, Mayor of Pocahontas, Arkansas, do here-by and henceforth issue this challenge to Tyrone the Cyclone. We want him or anybody else in Walnut Ridge who might be an even better arm wrestler to come to Pocahontas and arm wrestle Phil Hall, the Pocahontas Patriot. The winner will receive the beautiful belt known now and forever as the beautiful, the magnificent, the Putterham Prize."

Mama Regina hadn't finished her reading aloud before the sheriff began shaking his head side to side and shaking it so hard that I worried that his brains might rattle. "Ma'am, I sure hope you thank your lucky stars that I'm a patient man who respects age, 'cause I'm gonna explain to you what happened. Our mayor challenged your mayor to send the Cyclone or even somebody better . . . and since that didn't happen, our town wins and your town loses. Walnut Ridge has lost by default."

The lines across my grandmother's forehead deepened. "Whose fault? Are you blaming me, boy?"

"No, ma'am, not fault, *default*. Default! Your Cyclone loses by default because he was too much of a scaredy cat to even show up."

With her pointing finger, Mama Regina pointed again to the newspaper story. "Right here, where it say, *Or somebody better.* Well, that's me, 'cause I'm here and I'm that somebody better!"

This time, the sheriff didn't much bother to hide his smirk. "Ma'am, this is way too ridiculous to talk about."

Mr. Putterham waddled in front of the platform to say, "Yeah, well, little Granny. Listen to me and turn that old truck around and head on back to Walnut Ridge, where you belong!"

My grandmother bellowed back, "Don't you go calling

me granny, 'cause I sure ain't no kinda kin of yours!"

Mr. Putterham's face turned a slightly embarrassed pink. "Look, I don't want any more kin folks than I already have. Fact is, I don't really want any of them that I already have. So, now that that's settled, why don't you take your tinny old firetruck and siren yourself on out of here! We proud Pocahontians got us *real* business, important business, to take care of—an arm-wrestling prize, the Putterham Prize, to present."

"Who do you think you're ordering around, you piglet-stealing, heel-waddling penguin?" But as soon as my grandmother had said that, she stopped short, placing her hand over her mouth. It was as though she had said more, much more, than she had ever meant to say.

"Ohh," she said, looking every bit as sorry as I had ever seen her look. "If there are any real-live penguins out there among you all, hearing what I said—I sure didn't mean to compare you fine and noble birds with this poor, pathetic, pitiful Puttydutty of a human being. So, if I insulted any of you precious penguins, I really am sorry, 'cause I think you penguins are nice. Honest I do."

As soon as the storekeeper heard that, he started yelling. "The prize is *my* prize, got my name on it, the Putterham Prize! I'm saying that I don't care what you're saying, 'cause the prize is gonna stay here in Pocahontas, where it belongs."

When my grandmother protested that Pocahontas was

going back on its word, the merchant rushed over to the sheriff's side to whisper in his ear. Some of what he said I missed, but this part I heard and heard clearly: "Let the old girl arm wrestle Phil Hall . . . that a-way my beautiful Putterham Prize stays here with us . . . here in *our* town!"

While the sheriff kept repeating the word "Ridiculous," Judge Bassett (who folks say is still a judge even when she isn't wearing her black judge robes) walked up into the wrestler's ring to speak to the people. "If people can't go back on their words, then why should a town go back on its word? And it doesn't matter that Walnut Ridge sent us this poor, old thing as a joke, Pocahontas must still wrestle back. It's the law!"

All at once, everybody was belly laughing loudly at the thought that any town, even a town as nutlike as Walnut Ridge, would be silly enough to send a dear, sweet, little grandmother up against Pocahontas's mightiest arm warrior.

A man pushed his straw hat on the back of his head, while shouting out, "Letting the old lady fight our champ would be like sending a little baby out to fight the Gorilla Man."

A younger fellow standing right next to the straw-hat man added, "You can say that again. Letting her fight our champ would be as useless as trying to dig a tunnel with a toothpick."

And from some place deep in the crowd, this time it was a woman's voice that called out. "Wanna know what I think? I think that letting the little Walnut Ridge lady arm wrestle our mighty Phil would be every bit as crazy as trying to soak up the Black River with a sponge mop. Well, that's what I think!"

All the folks were laughing hard at those answers, but the loudest laughing might have been coming from Mr. Putterham himself. That in itself was a surprise, maybe the biggest surprise of all, since nobody had ever known the Puttydutty to laugh. Oh, he may have been caught smiling once or twice as he slipped thick wads of folding money into his cash register, but laughing? Never laughing. I'm certain that nobody had ever before seen him do that.

As the people shook their head in amazement, my grandmother sprang into the chair opposite Philip Hall. But, in the second after that, the Pocahontas Patriot was up on his feet, hollering out to anybody who'd listen. "No siree, I ain't about to arm wrestle no old lady. No honor and no glory in winning against no sweet, old grandmother!" And then the great Pocahontas Patriot began to stutter. " And . . . and . . . it . . . it could . . . be-e . . . worse . . . than . . . that."

The onlookers seemed shocked all the way from their pinky fingers down to their tiniest toes, asking, "What could be worse than that, eh, Phil?"

"What if just as the little granny and I grasped hands, I was suddenly struck down dead by lightning? BOOM! And I'd be as dead as any dead hero could be, but that ain't what folks would be saying! I'll tell you what folks would be saying, even as they carried my dead body to our church cemetery. They'd be laughing at the great Pocahontas Patriot who was beaten by a sweet old lady."

My grandmother called out loud enough for everyone to hear. "To tell the truth, I ain't all that sweet."

Then, from the audience came a voice that everybody recognized as the voice of not-so-old Miz Suby Sue Johnson. "Now that I've drunk enough water to float a boat, I'm feeling right fine and dandy again. And I've been thinking, since I'm a grandmother from Pocahontas, and she's a grandmother from Walnut Ridge, then we could arm wrestle each other for the greater glory of our own towns. Now, what could be fairer than that?"

My grandmother grumbled, "All this talking is wasting my time. Lots of Walnut Ridge folks are already gathering at my house to see the beau-ti-ful championship-wrestling belt that I'll be bringing home. Is it really all sparkly and shiny like folks say it is?"

As Suby Sue bounded up into the wrestler's ring, it was as though the whole town smiled together, and I know why. Suby Sue had enough fat, bone, and muscle on her to make two—no, better make that three—of my dear, little Mama Regina!

And of all the smilers, nobody was smiling wider than our Mr. Barnes, as he called out, "Poor, silly old soul, it's like an ant fighting an elephant."

But to nobody in particular, my grandmother kept right on complaining. "What's taking you slow-as-molasses Pocahontas people so long? Why, I should have already been halfway home with my pretty prize. Didn't I already tell you that from one side of Walnut Ridge to the other, folks are gathering at my house to see that Putterham Prize? Can't hardly wait to hear me tell them about one more of our fine ole victories over Pocahontas."

And it was what Mama Regina said that all at once turned the people's smiles into frowns. Seeing how upset everybody had suddenly become, the Pocahontas cheerleaders tried to turn the frowns back into smiles by cheering on the platform: "On to Vic-tory. On to Vic-tory. Fight, Pocahontas! Fight! Fight! FIGHT!!!"

As the two women seated themselves at the arm-wrestling table, Sheriff Miller began to look worried. He spoke to my grandmother as softly as he knew how to speak, but since he was never taught how to speak softly, everybody heard. "Ma'am, I'm afraid somebody might get hurt. Remember, brittle old bones break easily, so, if it's all the same to you, let's call the whole thing off."

Mama Regina sprang from her seat, while holding out

121

her hand for something, maybe it was for the prize. "That's fine and dandy with me, so now be a good boy and hand me over my pretty championship wrestler's belt and I'll be tooting on back home."

Suddenly, Sheriff Miller rubbed his forehead just as though something or somebody was giving him a headache. "Ma'am, I told you once. I told you twice. And now I'm telling you a third time: the championship belt ain't a present, it's a *prize*. A prize that has to be won!"

Mama Regina bobbed her head up and down just as though there was nothing in this world that she agreed with more. "I got me a waiting arm, and if Miz Suby Sue's got herself a waiting arm too, then we both be ready."

"Well, don't say you ain't been warned," said Sheriff Miller, looking as though he was being forced to do something he didn't want to do. "'Cause you've been warned, ma'am, you've sure enough been warned aplenty."

Giving a thumbs-up and ready sigh, my grandmother said, "Oh, quit your yipping and yapping and let's go!"

"Ohh, no . . . " the sheriff moaned, as he stretched out his arms toward the people just like he was begging for even the smallest scrap of their understanding. "Now, you know, folks, that what's going to happen next ain't what I *want* to happen. You all know. You all were here and you heard me plead with her to forget the arm wrestling so she won't break her old bones, but she won't do it. Not unless we give her what she didn't win and doesn't deserve."

The sheriff's words jabbed against my heart like a fighter's fist. She *could* get hurt. She would get hurt! Suby Sue is big and not-so-very old, while Mama Regina is small and oh-so-very old.

Without thinking, without even knowing that I was going to do what I did do, I found myself in the ring, whispering into my grandmother's ear. "Please, Mama Regina, please! You don't need their old championship belt. Why, they got prettier ones for sale right there inside at the Busy Bee Bargain Store. Really they do!"

Mama Regina smiled lovingly at me just as though my face was the world's most beautiful face. Then, as her fingers brushed lightly against my cheek, she said. "Why, ain't you one sweet thing to go worrying your pretty head about your old grandma? Beth babe, go back there among them watchers and find your ma and your pa. Then you close your eyes and press your head against them, and before you can say, 'Putterham Prize,' it'll all be over with."

I shook my head no. "But I can't leave you. Can't let Miz Suby Sue hurt you!"

Mama Regina's voice sharpened. "You hear me a-talking to you, girl? You do as I tell you, you hear?"

All at once, I felt tears, so many tears pressing up against my throat that I knew I couldn't speak. And to hide the tears that were now rolling like fat rain drops down my cheeks, I dropped my head against my chest as I jumped off the wrestler's platform.

But where were they? My family weren't where they had been. Reckon they couldn't stand watching any more than me. So, with my eyes clamped shut, I still couldn't stop the sheriff's voice from booming in my ears. "Ready, Ladies? Okay, elbows on the table . . . grasp hands . . . Ready . . . Set . . . GO!"

In the next moment—or maybe it was still that same moment—there was a crash, a terrible crash, that sounded like a dried-up old tree falling hard against the forest floor.

11

And the Winner Is . . .

From the large circling crowds that pressed against the wrestling ring came shrieks, screams, groans, and moans! It was an uproar so loud, so wild, that it sounded as though it could only come from a whole jungle full of ferocious beasts. Only it wasn't coming from jungle animals at all; it was coming from the people of Pocahontas.

And all together those groans-moans and shrieks-screams were scary enough to frighten even the longtime dead over there at the Old Rugged Church graveyard. Probably the only reason that I wasn't making a ruckus too was because my eyes were still as locked-down shut as the door of the Busy Bee Bargain Store after closing hours.

Hoping against hope that my grandmother's arm was still (right where it oughta be) attached to her body, I tried opening my eyes, but the covering eyelids couldn't go up. Maybe they *could,* but were, well, just way too frightened to even try. That's when I took a finger to each eyelid and in spite of my fears, in spite of what the eyelids wanted, I finally managed to push both those stubborn eyelids up. And it was then that I saw what was almost too unbelievable to believe.

And since what I saw, I couldn't believe, I blinked once and then again, and it was only then that I knew what I saw was for sure enough real. Mama Regina was flapping her arms around her head like an overexcited chicken, while at the same time do-si-do-ing around the wrestling ring and singing her made-up song.

> I kept my eyes on that pretty prize
> Knowing those Pocahontians would be surprised!
> But, no folks, I sure ain't gonna apologize
> As I go bringing home my Putterham Prize!

While my grandmother was singing, dancing, and, yes, arm flapping her way around and around the wrestling ring, two of Miz Suby Sue's daughters were helping their mama to her feet. Alisha, her third daughter, was kept real busy rubbing the pain away from her mama's aching right arm. But if Miz Suby Sue's arm felt pained and strained, it was nothing like the agony that was flashing across the merchant's face.

What I couldn't figure, though, is where all his hurting was coming from, 'cause Mr. Putterham's arm hadn't seen even a lick of arm wrestling. For one moment, two moments, three moments, four, his face looked sourer than a whole barrel full of sour pickles. But then, suddenly, all that changed.

Why his mood so quickly flipped from sour and flopped over to sweet, I didn't know. I only knew for sure that it certainly did flip flop. 'Cause at this very moment, the smiling storekeeper's face was every bit as happy as Philip Hall's face on the day he was chosen to be the top Tiger Hunter of the Tiger Hunters Club.

Fast walking his waddley walk to the very edge of the wrestling platform, the Puttydutty threw out his arms, while crying out to the people. "La-dies and gen-tle-men, since I am the great and generous giver of the famous Putterham Prize, it is, naturally enough, my duty to present the winner with this wonderful, sparkling championship belt. So, come on everybody. Let's all cheer the new champion arm wrestler!"

But, in spite of what the merchant asked folks to do, none of the sad and solemn watchers obeyed. To tell the truth, there wasn't even one cheer and certainly no hurrahs. At least not until he began telling them what came next.

"I know and you all know what anybody with eyes to see will surely know. And if you don't have good eyesight, then you can trust me, the most honest owner of the best store in Pocahontas. So, you all don't need me to tell you exactly who our winner is, 'cause it's plainer than the noses on your faces. And so to our new arm-wrestling champ, I say, trot yourself on over here, Miz Suby Sue Johnson, and accept what you just done fair and square won, the great and glorious Putterham Prize!"

The audience gasped in surprise, "Suby Sue?" Even I couldn't believe that the Puttydutty is giving the prize not to the winner but to the loser! Hearing his lying words made my mouth drop open so hard that I thought for a moment that it had come unhinged. But, thankfully, it didn't.

Although there had been not one single clap for my Walnut Ridge grandmother when the people thought that she had won, there were sure enough clapping aplenty for Pocahontas's hometown favorite. Fact is, looked like everybody (but me!) was wildly clapping, stomping, and cheering for honest-to-goodness real loser, Miz Suby Sue Johnson.

So much cheering and foot stomping that my first thought was that it sounded like a jillion thunder bolts had gone crashing across the heavens, and my second thought was that my grandmother was not being treated fairly.

But, wait, that's not really right! Now that I think about it, it was really the other way around. My first thought was that I was furious because my grandmother was being robbed of what was rightly hers, and my second thought was that all that unfairness was causing the heavens to go rumbling and rattling.

I was so mad that I didn't know what to do, but when I saw her shaking her bony fist in the face of the old Puttydutty, I knew that I didn't have to worry, 'cause nobody, and I mean *nobody*, pushes my grandmother around, at least not for long. "Come on and wrestle me, I dare you!" Mama Regina challenged him. "You piglet-stealing, walrus-waddling—"

Suddenly, she put her hand over her mouth just as though she had, without thinking, said something that she had never meant to say. "Oh, my goodness . . . Oh, my dear . . . If there are any of you dear walruses out there in the crowd who heard me compare you fine critters to this poor, pathetic Putterham of a person, then I hope you'll find it in your hearts to forgive me. 'Cause, the truth is, I love walruses, really and truly I doodelly, doodelly DO!"

As both Mr. Putterham and Sheriff Nathan Miller were signaling my grandmother with quick jerks of their heads as well as even quicker jerks of their thumbs to get her off the platform, old Mr. Simon Bartlett yelled out, "Go on back to your Walnut Ridge home, lady, 'cause your side lost and our side won! And that's all there is to that!"

And even Miz Suby Sue had something to say.

"Although I won, I believe, deep in my heart, that the contest was still mighty unfair to me! 'Cause I know that I could have won a little faster if I still hadn't been maybe the tiniest little bit thirsty. Yes siree bob-a-link, being thirsty that was my problem."

And the new winner didn't get her words out good before Mabel Ramsey added her thoughts. "You nutty Walnutters never play fair! And that's the truth! Trying to win against folks who are dying of thirst. Ain't nothing fair about that!"

In the next moment, I had bounded up on the wrestling platform to stand with my shoulder touching Mama Regina's shoulder, 'cause I couldn't bear the thought of her standing alone before the angry crowd! Didn't want her to think that everybody was against her and that nobody cared. Then, with my arm flopped over her shoulder and her arm flopped over my shoulder, we gave each other quick thanks-for-being-there squeezes.

I gazed across all those fine, familiar faces before shouting out my fury. "I have always been proud to be a Pocahontian, but today, right now, I ain't all that proud. The way you are treating my grandmother, the *real* true-blue winner, ain't right! Ain't fair, either! Maybe people from a lot of other towns don't think of us as big football, basketball, or baseball winners, but they haven't thought of us as cheaters, either. But maybe now they will."

Just then, Mama Regina leaned over to whisper something in my ear. I nodded my head in agreement before talking again to all the people. "Reckon you all know that my grandmother won fair and square. Even so, she just told me that she is willing to arm wrestle somebody else, anybody else, for the arm-wrestling championship."

As soon as the Puttydutty heard that, he began smiling again, just as though he knew something that nobody else knew. "Can't have a contest unless it's a fair-and-square contest," he said. "Fair and square, that's what I always say. So, if you want another chance to win at arm wrestling, old lady, then just to be fair, just to show you how good and kind we Pocahontians truly are, we're gonna give you your second chance."

Suddenly, he was pointing to someone out there in the crowd. "Leap yourself on up here, Leaping Leah Franklin! None of us will ever forget how you won the ladies' bull-roping contest at last year's county fair. Yes sir, for a person that's not even a guy person that was pretty fair roping. Got that nasty bull down in no time flat!"

With a single leap, Leah had sprung down hard on the platform. Beneath the sleeve of her denim shirt, her bulging arm muscles were every bit as hard to hide as the humps on a camel's back. But, as the Leaping Lady peered down at the little old lady from Walnut Ridge, she seemed to grow sadder and sadder.

Then, with tears bathing her eyes, the leaping one pleaded, "Ma'am, you're not just old. You're also so . . . so tiny, so delicate that I'm really afraid that somebody could just get themselves hurt. So, don't you think that . . . that someone could . . . could sorta . . . sorta, you know, just give up? Now don't you think that that would be nice?"

Those words hadn't come out of Leah's mouth good before Mama Regina did one of her happy little flapping-arms dances. "Oh, what a sweet idea, dear," she said, grabbing Leaping Leah's hand to shake on the agreement. "Ain't no need for you to get all hot, sweaty, and arm-sore over nothing. So, giving up now . . . well, I reckon that there ain't no finer time for you to give up, right here. Right now."

"But . . . but you don't understand," exclaimed Leah. "I don't want to give up. I want *you* to give up!"

My grandmother shrugged her shoulders just as though that was about the most surprising thing that she had ever in her life heard. "Well . . . well, now why on earth, dear, would I ever want to do that?"

"'Cause you could get hurt," squealed Leah. "I sure don't want to hurt you, but I'm so strong that well—I guess I could hurt you. Even though I'd try my best not to. Didn't anybody ever tell you that I could hurt you?"

Mama Regina smiled pleasantly before barking out her order. "Go sit yourself right down there at the wrestling table, dear, and don't go worrying your pretty head about hurting me. But you sure are a sweet young thing to go worrying."

The fact is that Leaping Leah wasn't the only one who was worrying about my grandmother. I was worried too, plenty worried. Maybe she did get a little lucky with another grandmother, but how in the world could she be lucky against the champ of all the bull ropers?

But, either Mama Regina was not worried or *pretended* not to be worried, 'cause she marched herself over and sat down at the wrestling table just like she owned it, the chairs, and all the land and lakes for at least a thousand miles. Pushing up her flowery sleeve where a knot of arm muscle should have been plainly seen wasn't seen. I mean, there was no grapefruit-sized muscle, no orange-sized muscle, and, sadly, not even a peanut-sized muscle.

Then, Leah sat down at the table directly across from my Mama Regina, and when she pushed up her sleeve, the crowd took one look and went, "Ohhhhh!" Then they went and took a second look at the leaper's greater-than-grapefruit-sized muscles and they went, "AHHHhhhhhhhhhhh!!!"

But when my grandmother grasped Leah's hand, the crowd moaned their sympathy. Here and there, I could hear people muttering things like, "Poor old lady." And then a man's voice, big and strong, called out, "Poor, old, pathetic thing! You better stop now or . . . you'll be sor-ry!"

The next thing I knew, I too was pleading with Mama Regina not to do what she was planning to do. "Please, you *know* you don't have to do this! It's not too late to change your mind. Who cares about an old belt, anyway? Please, Mama Regina, let Miz Leah have it. PLEASE!"

Even as Sheriff Nathan Miller nodded his get-ready sign toward the two women, I saw some concerned eyes in the audience already turning away. Away from what everybody knew would be an awful sight.

For moments, Sheriff Miller observed my grandmother with a worried look before calling on Mr. Simon Bartlett's son, Simon Bartlett Junior, to run over to Doc Tom Sabin's office. "Tell the doc that I want him here! Quick! Quick! And on the double!"

Then he turned to face the already seated Mama Regina and Leaping Leah. "Okay, ladies, listen up, 'cause first I'm gonna give you your rules. Elbows on the table . . . grasp hands . . . and then I'm gonna count to three and then I'll say, 'Go!' And when I say 'go,' you ladies do your best to pull your opponent's arm down to the table. Any questions?"

My grandmother smiled sweetly before asking even more sweetly, "If it's all the same to you precious Pocahontas people, do you think you could leave out the counting and just say 'go'? You see, I want to quicken this up. 'Cause my Walnut Ridge friends don't want to wait even a second more than they have to to see that pretty, pretty championship belt that I'm gonna be bringing on home."

The sheriff frowned at my grandmother before

answering her with his scariest guns-and-bullets voice. "Ma'am, as long as I'm sheriff of this county, we'll do what I say, and if I say I'm gonna count, then by gosh and by gumbo, I'm gonna COUNT!"

If it was at all possible to lock down my eyes even tighter than I had done before, then I had surely managed to do it. 'Cause no eyes in all of Pocahontas had ever been more securely latched, clasped, and padlocked down than mine are right now.

The onlookers as well as the two contestants listened as the sheriff spoke. "We Pocahontians have serious business here, folks, so without any more chitting and chatting or tittling and tattling, here we go. So, ladies, elbows on the table . . . grasp hands . . . one . . . two . . . three . . . GO!"

Then, in the next moment or maybe it was that same moment, there was a sound as loud and as frightening and as unexpected as a crack of whip, and an arm was heard smashing down hard against the solid wood table. But it wasn't until I heard the howls, moans, and groans of my Pocahontas town folks that I knew that I didn't have a thing to worry about. And so, without any push-ing or pulling help from my fingers, my eyes shot wide open.

The Leaper's head had dropped down on the table and her left arm was rubbing away the hurt. And that's when I felt even more confident than ever that it was okay to now glance over at my grandmother. And when I looked,

I saw that she was doing fine, actually a whole lot better than fine.

'Cause what she was doing was jumping up and down like the Easter bunny, while all the time peering hopefully into the face of the angry merchant. "So, I reckon I'll be taking my Putterham Prize now, Mr. Putterham. And I thanks you kindly. Sure do."

But the pickle-faced Putterham didn't answer, at least not exactly. Instead, he grabbed at his hair and, for a minute, I thought that he was going to pull it out, one gray strand at a time. But when I guessed that, I guessed wrong. Instead, what he did do was to holler at the winner and anybody else close enough to listen. "You think you won, old lady?! Is that what you are a-thinking?"

She fastened her hands against her hips in her I-ain't-fixing-to-take-no-nonsense-from-you stance. "I don't have to *think* I won, Mr. Merchant Man, 'cause I knows what I knows and I knows that I won. Why a person could be as dumb as an ox and as blind as a bat and still they'd know—know that I, the old Walnut Ridge granny, won!"

I took a step toward the storekeeper, while pleading, "Please give my grandmother what's hers. What she won!"

The storekeeper shook his sour head no. "Can't do that, can't give out my wonderful prize to someone who didn't win it fair and square!"

136

"But, Mama Regina did!" I protested. "She did win it, fair and square. Won the championship belt, not once but twice!"

"Look," he said, lifting the right hand of the still recovering Leaper high enough so all could see. "Tell me! Tell me, Beth Lambert, what do you see?"

"Only thing I see? Well, I reckon the only thing I see is that Miz Leaping Leah's hand is looking all worn out to a frazzle, as limp as the Pocahontas newspaper when it gets left out too long in the rain."

"No! Here! Look here!" Mr. Putterham cried out, while poking at two small orange-tan spots on the back of Leaping Leah's hand.

"Why, there ain't nothing there," I said, touching at the very spots he had been poking. "Nothing excepting two tiny little dots, probably freckles."

The Puttydutty shook my hand in excitement just as though my answer was really nothing short of amazing. "That's it! That's it! You *really* got it!"

"I did?"

"You certainly did!"

"Did what? What did I do?"

"Got it!"

"Uhh, what was it that I done got?"

As Mr. Putterham answered, it was clear that he wasn't talking only to me, but to the greater audience that was crowding around to watch and listen. "Sure you got it.

137

Didn't Beth get it, eh, folks? Didn't she catch on to just how heavy a freckle can be?"

"Well, no sir, I can't rightly say that I caught on to how heavy a freckle is, 'cause, well, I reckon I've never weighed one." And then I checked out my own Hershey chocolate–colored skin before adding, "Can't say that I've ever had a freckle either."

"AHHH—HA and AHHH-HO! Just what I expected, you thoughtless girl, you, Beth Lambert, you! Never giving a moment's worth of concern or consideration to the weight handicap that our lovely Leaping Leah had to overcome. Imagine that! Both of those heavy weight-bearing freckles pushing down on Leaping Leah's hand all the while she's trying her hardest to push up on the old one's hand. Who in their right mind would call that fair?"

"Wha—what silly thing are you saying, Mr. Putterham? Please, sir, I hope that you're not going to say what you might be thinking of saying next."

"All I'm saying, from the goodness and kindness of my heart," he insisted, "is that the old lady didn't win fair and square because our Leaping Leah had to overcome not one, but *two* terrible, weight-bearing hand freckles. And any arm wrestler will tell you that there's nothing like freckles to weigh a hand down."

"Well, I *don't* know that, 'cause freckles don't weigh a thing. So that's plumb crazy! Please just stop all this hanking and panking and give my grandmother what she already done won—the Putterham Prize!"

The old Puttydutty's face was becoming increasingly splotched with color. "What are you, Beth Lambert, some sort of freckle expert? That means that you know for sure and for certain, you know how heavy or how light a freckle is? Ain't you the same girl that stood in front of this assembly and admitted in front of us all that you had never in your life weighed a freckle? And, not to be nosy, but didn't you also admit in front of these Pocahontas people that you also have never even owned one? Not even *one* single, solitary freckle?"

Just as I opened my mouth to tell him what I thought about his whole wrong and wicked rules, I again felt my grandmother tugging on my sleeve. This time she whispered in my ear the same thing that she whispered in my ear the last time. Although I tried to persuade her differently, she was even more stubborn than me.

So I said to him, "Mr. Putterham, my grandmother agrees to arm wrestle one more time, only this time will be the last time, and this time you must promise that the *real* winner will take home the prize."

"Why, of course and of course," he said, as I watched his face begin to flip a little toward sweet. "I, Cyrus J. Putterham, Pocahontas's leading merchant, wouldn't want it any other way."

"You *really* mean it, Mr. Putterham?" I asked, while checking to see if his face was looking . . . well, maybe a little bit sincere. "So, you're saying that this time if my grandmother wins, you won't find any weird, made-up reasons that'll keep her from winning? And this time you'll actually let her go home with the Putterham Prize?"

His head was bobbing up and down faster than the needle on a sewing machine. "That is one promise that I won't have any trouble keeping."

A promise that the Puttydutty wouldn't have any trouble keeping? Could that really be true? I wondered if there was such a thing in all this world as a promise that he, a known promise-breaker, would keep? Oh, I guess if he promised that he'd take money for every sale or promised to chew bubble gum all day, every day, that he'd sure enough keep those promises all right.

But what about a different kind of a promise, a promise that's hard to keep? Would he keep that kind of promise, as well? It was too hard to know, so I decided that I just had to come on out and ask, "Mr. Putterham, would you stand there in front of everybody and give us your word that this is the last, the very last wrestling match? And that the winner, the *real* winner (not some made-up phony-baloney winner but the *real* winner) gets to take home the prize?"

Mr. Putterham spoke loud enough so that even folks at the far edges of the crowd clearly heard every word. "That's exactly the promise that I'm making in front of all the people. Besides, I've already run out of pretend reasons, tricks, and excuses. Only thing is, I don't have to worry about your grandmother winning. 'Cause this time Pocahontas is gonna bring out its finest wrestler."

For the life of me, I couldn't think who would be better than Leaping Leah. "Who is that, Mr. Putterham?"

The storekeeper proudly stuck out his chest just as though somebody was about to pin a medal on him. "Why, our town's all-time arm-wrestling champ, of course, of course. None other than him. The fearless . . . the unbeatable, Phil Hall, the one . . . the only Pocahontas Patriot!"

12

The Patriot and the Pirate

E ven as I watched, Philip Hall's eyes grew so large that, for the first time ever, I could see wide splashes of white surrounding his sweet and soft, marshmallowy brown eyes. And what with the storekeeper whispering to the Pocahontas Patriot in one ear and the sheriff whispering to him in the other, the look on Philip's face became more and more jiggily jangled. It looked to me that he'd have gladly taken off running if only the men would let him.

For long moments, the under-the-breath murmurings of the two men poured through poor Philip's ears until suddenly he yelped loudly enough for me to hear, "NO! Not with no old lady! No sir!!!"

Upon hearing his outburst, the shopkeeper's and the sheriff's expressions turned harder than peanut brittle, but it was Mr. Putterham who duck walked his way to the edge of the wrestling ring, threw out his arms, and began talking with the people. "My fellow citizens of this great and glorious town of Pocahontas, Arkansas, I am standing here in front of you all to tell you something that I sure-as-shooting do hate to tell you."

And the people called back, asking, "Well . . . what's the matter, Mr. Putterham?"

Looking very serious, he answered by angrily spitting out only three words, "The Pocahontas Patriot!"

All at once and all together, the people gasped, while sucking in almost enough air to cause a small hurricane. "Oh, no . . . not him! Not our Pocahontas Patriot!" It was as though Mr. Putterham's words were just about the most unbelievable thing that they had ever in their lives heard.

"Oh, yes, it's so sad, but oh-so true," he told them. "And what a sorrowful day for Pocahontas it is when the one person who we've all been counting on, and even depending on, to finally bring us a victory over Walnut Ridge has let us down. Oh, it's shameful, all right! Shameful! Phil Hall now refuses to do his duty and arm wrestle the granny so that we Pocahontians can keep here in our town what is rightfully ours: the Putterham Prize."

A boy's voice called out, "Say it ain't so, Phil Hall!" And then other folks began sounding off so that the whole town would know what was on their minds and in their hearts. I guess a lot of us recognized the voice of Miz Suby Sue, as she exclaimed, "Our Pocahontas Patriot would never let his hometown down! That can't be true!" And still others cried out, "No, not *our* Phil! Not *our* Phil Hall!"

Taking a step back, as though he wanted to be as far away from the people as possible, Philip Hall pleaded with his town to understand. "But . . . but us heroes don't ever go around arm wrestling with *girls*. Specially not with no girl that stopped being a girl a lot of long years ago."

Shoving Philip Hall off to one side, Sheriff Nathan Miller edged up closer to the crowd. "All you good people out there, please help the Pocahontas Patriot understand that it's wrong for him to refuse us now, now in our time of desperate need.

"So, all you good Pocahontas people, make him understand that if he doesn't do what we need him to do, then tonight every home in Walnut Ridge is going to rip with ridicule and roar with laughter. And don't nobody need to ask what town Walnut Ridge will be laughing at, 'cause we all know what town it's gonna be. Nobody's hometown but our hometown! From Walnut Ridge to Little Rock and as far east as Bangkok, people gonna laugh, ridicule, and mock."

Then it seemed as though everybody together was now taking the sheriff's advice and crying out their fury at

Philip Hall. They all did their very best to make him see that without the Pocahontas Patriot doing what only the Pocahontas Patriot can do, then they'd be known all around as a town full of losers and snoozers. One man with eyes damp with sadness asked, "Don't we Pocahontians also have the right to hold our heads up with a little pride? Don't we have that right, eh, Phil Hall?"

As Philip Hall listened to person after person explain how important he was to our town, the Pocahontas Patriot seemed to lose some fright and gain some pleasure. "Well, if you all really think that I'm the only one who can do it," he said at long last, "then I reckon I'm gonna have to do it."

Those words didn't get out of that boy's mouth good before everybody began noisily slapping one of their hands against their other hand. And all that racket and ruckus and clapping was for nobody but Philip Hall. Well, actually, my hands didn't do a thing, 'cause they were every bit as confused as my head. I didn't want Philip Hall to lose, but then again, I didn't want Mama Regina to lose, either. And it was important that she shouldn't lose. 'Cause I was afraid that if my grandmother lost, then it would mean, wouldn't it mean that she got hurt?

It was so hard to figure, 'cause there was something more here than even a contest between two people. It was, for sure, a contest between two towns. And it's how folks in this town think about folks in *that* town. Well, I don't know any nice way to say this, but the fact is that too many Pocahontas people believe that those people who live only seven miles up the road in Walnut Ridge are second cousins to the devil himself. I hope nobody asks me why I believe that, 'cause if they did I'd have to tell them the truth. And the truth is that we Pocahontians are jealous 'cause their teams are always better than ours.

Once (and I'll never forget this), I told Philip Hall that I believe that the real answer to why we're always losing was because they always play better. And all I said was that pure and shining truth, but that didn't stop Philip Hall from being so mad that he almost jumped out of his skin and down my throat while calling me "a traitor to my own people." So, although the truth might not always be appreciated in his town, I do think it would be really nice if, for a change, Pocahontas could win over Walnut Ridge.

But if Philip Hall didn't win, that would be really bad, 'cause then that boy wouldn't hardly be Philip Hall anymore. Not just losing, but also losing to a Walnutter, and a granny Walnutter at that. Why, he'd spend the rest of his natural life searching for a rock big enough to crawl under. Oh, I can see it all now, the confidence squeezed right out of him, a lot like the way my ma squeezes every drop of juice out of an orange. And after only one of her squeezes, about the only thing left is the peel. What, I worried, would be left of Philip Hall after all the pride is pushed and pressed out of him?

One good thing, though, about Mama Regina is that win or lose, her self-confidence would stay the same, 'cause that woman has more spirit than those cheerleaders as they go swishing this a-way and swashing that a-way.

I had still other muddying thoughts that still needed clearing up, but they were interrupted by the booming commands of our sheriff. "The Pocahontas Patriot and the Walnut Ridge granny will now take their places at the arm-wrestling table. I will give both contestants the rules of the arm-wrestling contest, and after you've both heard all the rules, then I'll let the contest begin. Any questions?"

No sooner had the sheriff said that than my Mama Regina began flip-flopping her hand like a flag on a windy, windy day. Sheriff Miller sighed wearily just as though my grandmother had suddenly sapped all the energy from his body. "You don't really have yourself a question, now do you, ma'am?"

"Oh, yes, yes, indeed. Seeing as how I've already heard the rules two times and seeing as how your Pocahontas Pirate—"

"Not pirate!" interrupted the sheriff. "Patriot, ma'am. Pocahontas *Patriot!*"

"Oh, piddle-paddle," said Mama Regina, as her hand made little downward pats, just as though she was patting down the air or maybe even only patting away little bits of the lawman's nonsense. "Pirate, patriot, what's the difference?"

Sheriff Miller shook his pointing finger at her and didn't stop wagging it, all the while he explained. "What's the difference? You're asking me, what's the difference? All the difference in the world, 'cause a pirate sails the seas in pirate ships to steal from others, while a patriot is a hero who'll risk his life to save people. And in this case, Phil Hall is the patriot, and we Pocahontians are his people. Now, if there are no more questions," he said, looking directly at Mama Regina. "And I'm certain that there are no more questions, I'll now give the rules."

At that my grandmother was again waving her hand for attention, only now she was also jumping up and down in her seat. "Reckon the question that needed answering never got answered, 'cause I never got through asking it. Now, ain't that the gospel truth?"

Through clenched teeth and a smile that looked phony, the sheriff answered, "So, ask the question! Ask it!"

If my grandmother had smiled sweetly before, it was no way as sweet as the smile that she was smiling now. "What I've been trying to ask is this: since I've heard the rules two times and since this here Pocahontas Pirate has heard the rules two—"

The sheriff interrupted, "Don't you *ever* again call him a pirate, 'cause like I told you before, he's no pirate, he's a *patriot!*"

"Patriot," continued Mama Regina. "Yes, indeedy, sir, patriot. Well, since that patriot over there has already heard the rules two times and since I've already heard the rules two times, don't you think we could speed things up? Do away with hearing them rules again? We gotta hurry this arm wrestling up. Don't you know? 'Cause all my Walnut Ridge friends are waiting to see the Putterham Prize, and they are all so anxious they can barely wait."

The sheriff rubbed his forehead just as though he either already had a headache or was just about to get one. "Ma'am, if my patience with you were a rope, it would be all ragged and frayed. So ragged and frayed that if you put even one more thing on it—even a feather—it would snap. So, please don't ask me any more questions, just do as I say, and maybe that'll keep my patience from SNAPPING!"

My grandmother's face became all kind and caring. "Don't want to upset you, Mr. Sheriff, sure don't," she said, as she quietly sat herself down at the wrestling table. I then glanced at Philip Hall just in time to see him smile up at the glittering championship belt that Mr. Putterham was holding high in his hands. And, unless I'm really really wrong, our Pocahontas Patriot

149

did a little more than just smile at that belt. He also—was it at all possible that he actually winked at the Putterham Prize? Seemed like his way of telling the belt not to worry, 'cause soon the belt was gonna be his and his alone.

"Elbows on the table . . . " ordered the lawman. "Grasp hands . . . one . . . two . . . three . . . GO!!!"

Then, just at the exact moment that the sheriff called "go," I turned my head because I couldn't bear seeing my grandmother hurt any more than I could bear to see my grandmother, Philip Hall, or even our own town lose. So, whoever did win, I knew that I would be feeling pretty sad and sorry for the one who lost.

Although my eyes might have been shut down, my ears were as wide open for hearing as ever, but this time I didn't hear what I've heard twice before, the slamming down of one arm against the arm-wrestling table. So that was it. The struggle was still going on, as sometimes the people said, "Ooooohh," and at other times the people said, "Ahhhhh."

And then, finally, I heard it. The sound of an arm flopped down against the wrestling table followed by one great, pain-wracked groan coming from the people, all the people. I wondered if everybody could have come down with the same exact pain at the same exact moment. But my second thought was that my first thought didn't make much sense, 'cause not even

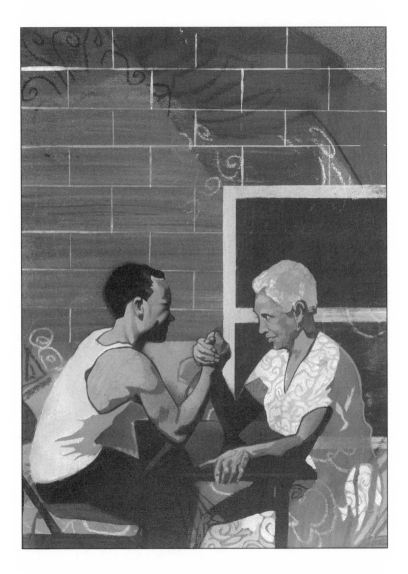

Sidewalk Sam's fieriest chilidogs could have done that to so many so quickly.

No, somebody had just won the great arm-wrestling championship, and from the sounds of all the people's agony, it didn't take me any more thinking to know exactly who that somebody might be.

13

The Fun Maker

As my eyes flashed open, I saw her doing her winner's dance around and around the ring, throwing her arms to the heavens, all the while singing her very own song of victory:

> I kept my eyes on that pretty prize
> Knowing you Pocahontians would be
>   surprised!
> But I ain't gonna cry or apologize
> As I come bringing home my Putterham Prize!

Mama Regina's happiness made me happy until I looked at Philip Hall, who looked as powerfully pitiful, as though he had let down the whole world. And just one quick glance at all that unhappiness was enough to make me unhappy too.

Just then, the Puttydutty heel walked his way over to the edge of the ring, where he spoke to all those sad-eyed onlookers. "Well, I know what you folks are thinking, but I'm thinking that you folks ain't thinking right. No siree, if you are thinking that our Pocahontas Patriot lost to the old granny there, then I'm telling you—telling you all to go put on your thinking caps and go think again! And again!"

Miz Suby Sue sputtered, "But . . . but we saw—with our own eyes, we saw the granny—"

"You ain't seen diddily-squat," argued the storekeeper.

"We ain't?" asked Miz Suby Sue. "You mean . . . I ain't?"

"No, ma'am, you ain't," he thundered before going on with his explaining. "'Cause the contest was unfair to the Pocahontas Patriot, 'cause he didn't know that the granny was going to smash his arm down on the wrestling table just when he least expected it. Did you know that, Phil?"

Slowly Philip Hall raised his drooping head. "What?" he asked, while looking as though he was still in the middle of a very bad dream. "Did I know what?"

"See! See!" said the Puttydutty, just as though he had won a great victory. "What did I tell you? What did I tell you?! Phil Hall not only didn't know *that*. He also didn't know *what!* Nothing fair about that!"

"It sure sounds fair to me!" I yelled out, but neither he

nor anybody else paid any attention.

"So, being the fair-minded fair person that I am," the merchant reminded us, "I, Cyrus J. Putterham, am willing, from the goodness of my heart, to give the little granny still another chance to win, another chance to bring home the wonderful, the magnificent Putterham Prize!"

As I looked out over the people, I saw that Miz Suby Sue's head, like so many others, were now slowly bobbing up and down in agreement. And, at the same time, my head was angrily shaking side to side in disagreement.

Even so, the Puttydutty went right on explaining. "So, little granny, out of the fairness of my fair heart, I'm gonna give you still another chance to win the Putterham Prize, only this time you'll have to win it against Homer."

"Homer?" my grandmother asked, while managing to sound every bit as surprised as she looked.

"Known far and wide," answered the storeowner, "as Pocahontas's strongest (and most stubborn) mule."

Miz Suby Sue stopped her gently agreeable nods to call out, "Now, I know that that ain't right, 'cause Homer has four powerful legs all right, but not a single arm for arm wrestling."

The merchant, wearing his best I-know-everything expression, answered, "This *new* contest for the Putterham Prize is going to be a little different, 'cause this will be a *pulling* contest. The Pocahontas Mule will try to pull the Walnut Ridge granny and the Walnut Ridge granny will try to pull the Pocahontas Mule. Now, talk about fair! What could be fairer than that? Somebody go bring Homer from the pasture and let the contest begin!"

I know that I've been mad before, but never in my life have I been any madder than I am now. Right now! Right this minute! I ducked around in front of Mr. Putterham and from the height of this platform, I looked down at all those people who were now looking up at me.

So much needed saying, and all these things and more were banging and bumping around inside my brain. So, where do I start? And where will I end? The people's eyes never seemed to leave me as one moment was followed by another, which was followed by another until finally, I thought of my beginning. And so I began, "I know that you all are upset that Philip Hall didn't win the arm-wrestling contest, but the truth is, he didn't . . . didn't win."

I twirled around to set a steel-like stare on Mr. Putterham. "And all of your plotting and scheming ain't gonna change one simple fact: my grandmother won that arm-wrestling contest! She won it, not one time or two times, but *three* times! And it's not fair and it's not right and it ain't even honest, either, that you want to make her go tugging on some old mule just to get what she's already done three times won: the Putterham Prize."

Mr. Putterham shook an angry fist in my direction.

"Now, you listen here. Just who do you think you are, Beth Lambert?"

"No sir, Mr. Putterham, it's time, way past time, that you listened! It ain't no disgrace for Pocahontas to lose some football, baseball, and basketball games. And it ain't even no disgrace that our very own Pocahontas Patriot lost to the Walnut Ridge granny. But it *is* a disgrace to cheat anybody out of what is rightfully theirs!"

Mr. Putterham gave me a shove against my shoulder. "Okay, now girl, get! I've been as nice to you as anyone could ever be. I've let you say your little piece, and you can't say that I didn't. But now you just skip along (or whatever it is that you foolish girls do!) and leave these important decisions to us grown-ups. You hear?"

"But . . . but I haven't finished saying what I came to say."

"Oh, yes, you're finished all right! Now get!" he said, all the while his thumb pointed the way off the platform as though I couldn't find the right direction without his not-at-all-helpful help.

Then from the people came their calls, "Let Beth talk!" And from at the edge of the crowd there were loud chants of, "Talk, Beth, talk!" Even the voice of Miz Suby Sue rang out clearly, "If Beth Lambert has something to say, then, by golly and by gump, you let her say it! You hear?"

Hugging the championship belt to his chest, the storekeeper backed away as he called out to anyone

157

who'd listen, "Okay, let her waste your time! You think I care? I don't care! Not me, 'cause I'm Pocahontas's leading merchant! And it was me who out of the kindness of my heart donated the Putterham Prize, and don't none of you go forgetting it!"

As folks snickered at Mr. Putterham, I took a step forward. "Well, I heard some of you talking, telling others that the Walnut Ridge granny must have got her strength from magic tricks or maybe even from witchcraft. But folks who are saying that are saying a lie." Mama Regina shouted out her encouragement. "Tell them, Beth! You tell them!"

"Reckon I know the truth and I'm gonna tell it to you now. It all happened after my grandfather died and my grandmother was left alone to run their apple farm. Maybe some of you know it? The Good Eating Apple Farm?"

Here and there a few voices called out that they did know it, and I took that as encouragement to go on, and so I did. "Well, a farm can raise the best apples in all the world, but if the farmer can't get those apples to a place where people will buy them, then what good are they? No good. So, without my grandfather around to lift those heavy apple-filled wood crates and put them up onto the truck, my grandmother had to do it. Only she couldn't.

"Those crates were too heavy, and she didn't know what to do. So one day, after her eyes got too tired and

158

too scratchy for any more crying, Mama Regina decided that she'd have to try something else, something a lot more useful than crying. And so she did. She went to work building up her strength.

"And every morning before the sun came up, she'd go into her apple orchard to practice lifting the empty wood crates. And finally, when she could do that okay, she practiced lifting the crate with only one apple inside, then the crate with two apples inside, and then three, and four, and on and on and on and on. After many many more weeks, my grandmother was lifting those apple crates filled to overflowing as fast as anyone. Ask anybody from around Walnut Ridge and they'll tell you that nobody can do it faster.

"So, to all of you who think that she couldn't do it without tricks or magic, then I guess you all know better now. 'Cause the real answer is a simple answer: my Mama Regina became strong just one apple at a time."

I glanced over at Mama Regina, who seemed to have suddenly lost her natural winning ways and was just now looking as shy as a little lost lamb. She creeped up to my side, saying, "Awww, goodness gracious . . . it wasn't hardly nothing. Nothing nobody else couldn't have done!"

Slowly my head bounced up and down as I thought over her words. "I reckon that my grandmother is right when she says that it's something that anybody could do . . . only, the thing is, nobody else *did* do it. Just my grandmother, knowing that she had to be as strong as the strongest of men, went to all the trouble and all the struggle to make herself *that* strong. As strong as most any man!"

And it was after I spoke that I noticed something very strange, well, maybe not strange, but something very unexpected, was happening. All those people out there were no longer looking mad or even tight and tense. Actually, their faces, every one of those faces, were becoming as relaxed as a sweetly sleeping baby's.

Then I heard it—those Tat-TAT-TATTING noises, just like when a hard rain strikes a tin roof, only the skies weren't raining rain, but shining with sunflowery yellow sunshine. And so, no, it wasn't raining at all, but something was coming down that was so much more surprising. It was . . . applause. Applause for my grandmother! Was it possible that now that they understood Mama Regina more, that they hated her less? Was it at all possible that they didn't hate her at all?

As I looked across all those smiling faces, my heart flooded over with happiness, 'cause I was never, in all my born days, prouder to be a Pocahontian. Maybe only Pocahontas people had hearts big enough to cheer a victory that wasn't a Pocahontas victory. And a Walnut Ridge victory at that! Then, from the far edge of the watchers, a man's strong voice rang out, "Okay, Putterham, no more trickery. Go ahead and do it. Give the lady her prize!"

Upon hearing that, Mr. Putterham squeezed the belt so tightly to his chest that he would have squeezed the life out of it, had there been any life in it. But none of that stopped others from taking up the chant: "Give granny her prize! Give granny her prize! Give granny her prize!"

As the chanting grew ever louder, the storekeeper's face turned the color of ripe watermelon and his lower lip pushed out far enough to make a right nice shelf. Then, with a sudden, quick shove, Mr. Putterham jammed the championship belt into the surprised hands of Philip Hall. "I'm giving my famous Putterham Prize to the great winner of the arm-wrestling contest, the one and only Pocahontas Patriot, Champion Phil Hall!"

Moments passed and more moments passed as Philip Hall caressed the belt of champions first with his eyes and then with his hands. And anyone watching would know and know at once what I know. That if Philip Hall ever in his life loved a thing, it was *this* thing. This belt that he would hold and cherish for now and for forever.

Only, strangely enough, his head now seemed to be moving in the wrong direction. I mean, not up and down like, "Yes, yes, this is mine, all mine." But more side-to-side, like to say, "No, no, this isn't mine, 'cause it doesn't belong to me." Then, turning to face the storekeeper, he said in a voice both loud and clear, "I never wanted you to *give* me the Putterham Prize, Mr. Putterham. I wanted to win it, and I tried my best to, but I . . . but I didn't."

Then, looking like a prince who was presenting a great gift of gold to his queen, Philip Hall carried the champion's prize to Mama Regina. "Reckon I didn't win it, granny," he told her. "You did."

She cradled the belt in her arms, giving it the same loving look that she gives me, Luther, Annie, and our little Baby Benjamin. And all that love she showed made me feel all warm and comfortable inside until I made the mistake of looking over at Philip Hall. And although I can tell you, for sure and for certain, that that boy is no crybaby, just one look at his face showed me something that I didn't ever want to see.

Only a glance, and a little one at that, and I could tell that in a place deep within him, a place that nobody else could see, he felt so very sad. Actually way too sad, even, for tears. Poor, poor Philip Hall. I wish I could make him understand that he didn't fail Pocahontas. Fact is, nobody could have beaten my Mama Regina. I wanted to pat his shoulder and tell him not to feel so bad, and maybe even remind him that maybe someday, on some faraway day, he might even smile once more.

After all, who else would have had the courage that he had? Going against the Puttydutty and even going against the sheriff to say no to a prize that for one never-to-be-forgotten moment really was his, all his?

As soon as the applause for my grandmother died down, I once again did the Miss Johnson thing and raised my hand for quiet, and then it happened. There was quiet, and that's when I called out to the people. "My grandmother wants you to know that she appreciates all your good will, and I thank you too, 'cause the truth is, there's no better arm wrestler anywhere than my Mama Regina."

And when I said that, everybody began applauding all over again. So much so that it took three more Miss Johnson–style arm raisings before the folks settled down long enough to listen to the rest of it. "Well, I was thinking, hoping, that we could also honor a person, not because that person won, but because he was honest enough to admit that he didn't."

Mama Regina began tugging at my sleeve. "You is talking about the Pocahontas Pirate, ain't you?"

"Uh, well, yes, only it's the Patriot, Grandma. The Pocahontas *Patriot.*"

She gave me one of her don't-you-go-wasting-my-time looks. "That's what I said, the Pocahontas Patriot. Beth, babe, you better go wash the wax out of your ears."

People laughed at that, and even though I was embarrassed, at least about the ear thing, I reckon that I laughed too.

Then, all at once, her face changed just as though a new idea had come barging its way on through. That's when she whispered something strange in my ear.

And I whispered back, "But, you don't mean now? You

don't want me to get it *now*?"

"Ain't no better time than this time, Beth. So, go get it now."

Even as I jumped off the platform and raced straight for that polished ax that hung on the side of the firetruck, I wondered if I had heard right. "You don't mean this, Mama Regina?" I asked, while raising up the hatchet to her eye level.

"'Course I mean *that!*," she said, while taking it from me before going back to her conversation with the people. "This here Putterham Prize is way too big a prize to wrap around my waist. Enough belt here to make three, maybe more, trips around my middle. So if it's all the same to you, folks, I was thinking . . . ," she said, while pausing long enough to look straight out at all the people who were now looking back with so much interest that not a person there would for a second dare to turn away.

"Well, what were you thinking, sweet granny?" asked the Puttydutty, while grabbing out for the trophy.

"Not so dangbang fast!" Mama Regina answered, while moving the belt beyond his greedy grasp. "I ain't thinking of giving *you* what I already done fair-and-square got, but I was thinking that this here belt *does* needs sharing. But not with you! Anyways, I don't have to wear this prize around my waist, 'cause it's way too big for me, but I can put it on my shelf or hang it on my wall next to a pretty picture."

And as soon as she said that, my grandmother laid the belt flat across the wrestling table and, without another word, she took her ax and whacked the belt into two equal parts. Then, with all the majesty of royalty, Mama Regina handed over half a belt to a dazzled Philip Hall. "Reckon this part of the Putterham Prize will always stay right here in Pocahontas, right here with the Pocahontas Pirate."

All together and all at the same time, the sheriff and the people shouted out their correction. "Patriot, Granny! *Patriot!!!*"

"And I ain't giving it to him 'cause I'm a sweet old lady either," said Mama Regina, ignoring the correction. "'Cause my granddaughter, Beth, will tell you the truth. Tell you that I ain't all that sweet."

All the while that people were laughing with Mama Regina, I was smiling my proudest smile; even so, she went on explaining right through all that happy laughter. "That pirate boy—"

"Patriot, granny, PATRIOT!" the people screamed.

"Yep, the Patriot, him, too!" she said. "He had the prize all to himself, but he didn't keep it. Gave it to me 'cause his heart told him that it was the right thing to do."

Suddenly everybody was doing it, applauding their hardest both for my grandmother and for Philip Hall, but there wasn't one person out there who was clapping with any more racket than me! Finally, when the noise fell away, Miz Suby Sue yelled out, "How come you didn't ax that belt into three pieces, granny? That a-way part of the prize could go to Pocahontas's best fun maker, our Beth. Beth Lambert!"

That's when I heard those four oh-so-familiar voices, those very pretty Pretty Penny voices piercing through the noise of the crowd as they went chanting, "Go, Pret-ty Pen-ny . . . Go PRET-ty PEN-ny! GO! GO!! GO!!! Yea, BETH! Yea, LAMBERT! Yea! Yea! BETH LAMBERT!!!"

And amid all that hollering, clapping, and foot stomping for me, there was nobody who was doing it with more noisy enthusiasm than Mr. Philip Marvin Hall himself. The cutest boy in the J. T. Williams School and the bravest Tiger Hunter of them all! One of us smiled first, I reckon it was me, and then he smiled back his very shiniest glad-to-be-alive smile.

It was then that he went and did something especially peculiar for Philip Hall. Slowly, he took one step, two steps, and finally a third step before holding out his hand toward me. As we shook hands and our eyes went eyeball to eyeball, he asked, "Besides the Cyclone lie, ain't there something else that you ought to own up to? Something else that you want to finally get around to truth telling about?"

I nodded yes, 'cause I couldn't stop remembering that not-at-all-true thing I had once told Philip. But all I could do was to nod again, because when a person does wrong, it's easier to admit it with your moving head than it is with your moving tongue. Thinking back, I remember how easily that lie floated up from my mouth, and now I'm thinking how hard it is to stand here and admit it.

Even so, I finally heard myself doing it. "Well, back when I told you that I wasn't in Walnut Ridge a week before I had already forgotten your name . . . well, that was one, too. A lie."

Somewhere along the way, I don't exactly remember when, our hands stopped shaking. And yet, his hand didn't let go, but kept on hand-holding mine. Is there, I wondered, an exact moment when hand-shaking turns into hand-holding?

Funny thing was, he kept on holding on, even as he asked, "You mean to say . . . you didn't? Didn't forget my name?"

I squeezed his hand. "Nahh, I reckon that was the biggest, fattest, baddest lie of them all, 'cause the truth is . . . I couldn't—I wouldn't! No, I'll never forget your name, Philip Hall!"